For Faith & Lily,
the next generation of Gallagher Girls

Acknowledgements

I'm tremendously grateful to all the people who have helped bring the Gallagher Girls to life–especially the wonderfully talented Donna Bray, whose support has meant more than I can ever say. Also, I owe a great deal to Arianne Lewin and the entire Hyperion team of whom I am continually in awe. I would also like to thank my agent, Kristin Nelson; also, Jennifer Lynn Barnes and Karen Walters for all of their incredible support. And, of course, I owe everything to my family, who have always been there for me. And last but certainly not least, I thank all the wonderful readers, like Victoria Sperow, Kami Elrod, Kelsey Wehmhoff, Paul Hollingsworth, Neha Mahajan, and Kara McBrayer, who make it all worthwhile.

ORCHARD BOOKS
338 Euston Road, London NW1 3BH
Orchard Books Australia
Level 17/207 Kent Street, Sydney, NSW 2000

First published in 2007 in the United States by Hyperion Books for Children
This edition published by Orchard Books in 2015

ISBN 978 1 40830 952 0

18

Printed and bound by CPI Group (UK) Ltd, Croydon, CR0 4YY

The paper and board used in this book are made from wood from responsible sources.

Orchard Books is an imprint of Hachette Children's Group and published by The Watts Publishing Group Limited, an Hachette UK company.

www.hachette.co.uk

Cross my heart
and hope to spy

Ally Crter

ORCHARD

Chapter 1

"Just be yourself," my mother said, as if that were easy. Which it isn't. Ever. Especially not when you're fifteen and don't know what language you're going to have to speak at lunch, or what name you'll have to use the next time you do a "project" for extra credit marks. Not when your nickname is "the Chameleon".

Not when you go to a school for spies.

Of course, if you're reading this, you probably have at least a Level Four clearance and know all about the Gallagher Academy for Exceptional Young Women – that it isn't *really* a boarding school for privileged girls, and that, despite our gorgeous mansion and manicured grounds, we're not snobs. We're spies. But on that January day, even my mother...even my *headmistress*...seemed to have forgotten that when you've spent your whole life learning fourteen different languages and how to completely alter your appearance using nothing but nail clippers and shoe polish, then being yourself gets a little harder – that we Gallagher Girls are really far better at being someone else.

(And we've got the fake IDs to prove it.)

My mother slipped her arm around me and whispered, "It's going to be okay, kiddo," as she guided me through the crowds of shoppers that filled Pentagon City Mall. Security cameras tracked our every move, but still my mother said, "It's fine. It's protocol. It's normal."

But ever since I was four years old and inadvertently cracked a Sapphire Series NSA code my dad had brought home after a mission to Singapore, it had been pretty obvious that the term *normal* would probably never apply to me.

After all, normal girls probably love going to the mall with their pockets full of Christmas money. Normal girls don't get summoned to Washington D.C. on the last day of the winter holidays. And normal girls very rarely feel like hyperventilating when their mothers pull a pair of jeans off a rack and tell a sales assistant, "Excuse me, my daughter would like to try these on."

I felt anything but normal as the sales assistant searched my eyes for some hidden clue. "Have you tried the ones from Milan?" she asked. "I hear the European styles are very flattering."

Beside me, my mother fingered the soft denim. "Yes,

I used to have a pair like this, but they got ruined at the cleaners."

And then the sales assistant pointed down a narrow hallway. A hint of a smile was on her face. "I believe dressing room number *seven* is available." She started to walk away, then turned back to me and whispered, "Good luck."

And I totally knew I was going to need it.

We walked together down the narrow hall, and once we were inside the dressing room my mother closed the door. Our eyes met in the mirror, and she said, "Are you ready?"

And then I did the thing we Gallagher Girls are best at – I lied. "Sure."

We pressed our palms against the cool, smooth mirror and felt the glass grow warm beneath our skin.

"You're going to do great," Mom said, as if being myself wouldn't be so hard or so terrible. As if I hadn't spent my entire life wanting to be *her*.

And then the ground beneath us started to shake.

The walls rose as the floor sank. Bright lights flashed white, burning my eyes. I reached dizzily for my mother's arm.

"Just a body scan," she said reassuringly, and the elevator continued its descent further and further beneath the city. A wave of hot air blasted my face like the world's biggest hair dryer. "Biohazard detectors," Mom explained as we continued our smooth, quick ride.

Time seemed to stand still, but I knew to count the seconds. One minute. Two minutes…

"Almost there," Mom said. We descended through a thin laser beam that read our retinal images. Moments later, a bright orange light pulsed, and I felt the elevator stop. The doors slid open.

And then my mouth went slack.

Tiles made of black granite and white marble stretched across the floor of the cavernous space like a life-sized chess-board. Twin staircases twisted from opposite corners of the massive room, spiralling forty feet to the second storey, framing a granite wall that bore the silver seal of the CIA and the motto I know by heart:

And ye shall know the truth, and the truth shall set you free.

As I stepped forward I saw elevators – dozens of them – lining the wall that curved behind us. Stainless steel letters above the elevator from which we'd just emerged spelled out WOMEN'S WEAR, MALL. To the right, another was labelled MEN'S ROOM, ROSLYN METRO STATION.

A screen on top of the elevator flashed our names. RACHEL MORGAN, DEPARTMENT OF OPERATIVE DEVELOPMENT. I glanced at Mom as the screen changed. CAMERON MORGAN, TEMPORARY GUEST.

There was a loud ding, and soon DAVID DUNCAN, IDENTIFYING CHARACTERISTICS REMOVAL DIVISION was emerging from the elevator labelled SAINT SEBASTIAN

CONFESSIONAL, at which point I totally started freaking out – but not in the Oh-my-gosh-I'm-in-a-top-secret-facility-that's-three-times-more-secure-than-the-White-House sense. No, my freak-outedness was purely of the This-is-the-coolest-thing-that's-ever-happened-to-me sense, because, despite three and a half years of training, I'd temporarily forgotten why we were here.

"Come on, sweetie," Mom said, taking my hand and pulling me through the atrium, where people climbed purposefully up the spiralling stairs. They carried newspapers and chatted over cups of coffee. It was almost…normal. But then Mom approached a guard who was missing half his nose and one ear, and I thought about how when you're a Gallagher Girl, normal is a completely relative thing.

"Welcome, ladies," the guard said. "Place your palms here." He indicated the smooth counter in front of him, and as soon as we touched the surface I felt the heat of the scanner that was memorising my prints. A mechanical printer sprang to life somewhere, and the guard leaned down to retrieve two badges.

"Well, Rachel Morgan," he said, looking at my mother as if she hadn't been standing right in front of him for a full minute, "welcome back! And this must be little…" The man squinted, trying to read the badge in his hand.

"This is my daughter, Cameron."

"Of course she is! She looks just like you." Which just

9

proved that whatever terrible nose incident he'd experienced had no doubt affected his eyes, too, because while Rachel Morgan has frequently been described as beautiful, *I* am usually described as nondescript. "Strap this on, young lady," the guard said, handing me the ID badge. "And don't lose it – it's loaded with a tracking chip and half a milligram of C-4. If you try to remove it or enter an unauthorised area, it'll detonate." He stared at me. "And then you'll die."

I swallowed hard, then suddenly understood why take-your-daughter-to-work day was never really an option in the Morgan family.

"OK," I muttered, taking the badge gingerly. Then the man slapped the counter, and – spy training or not – I jumped.

"Ha!" The guard let out a sharp laugh and leaned closer to my mother. "The Gallagher Academy is growing them more gullible than it did in my day, Rachel," he teased, then winked at me. "Spy humour."

Well, personally, I didn't think his "humour" was all that funny, but my mother smiled and took my arm again. "Come on, kiddo, you don't want to be late."

She led me down a sunny corridor that made it almost impossible to believe we were underground. Bright, cool light splashed the grey walls and reminded me of Sublevel One at school…which reminded me of my Covert Operations class…which reminded me of finals week… which reminded me of…

Josh.

We passed the Office of Guerrilla Warfare but didn't slow down. Two women waved to my mother outside the Department of Cover and Concealment, but we didn't stop to chat.

We walked faster, going deeper and deeper into the labyrinth of secrets, until the corridor branched and we could either go left, towards the Department of Sabotage and Seemingly Accidental Explosions, or right, to the Office of Operative Development and Human Intelligence. And despite the FLAME-RESISTANT BODYSUITS MANDATORY BEYOND THIS POINT sign marking the hallway to my left, I'd much rather have gone in that direction. Or just back to the shopping mall. Anywhere but where I knew I had to go.

Because even though the truth can set you free, that doesn't mean it won't be painful.

"My name is Cammie."

"No, what's your *full* name?" asked the man in front of the polygraph machine, as if I weren't wearing the aforementioned (and supposedly nonexplosive) name badge.

I thought about my mother's words of wisdom and took a deep breath. "Cameron Ann Morgan."

The room around me was completely bare, except for a stainless steel table, two chairs, and a mirror made of one-way glass. I probably wasn't the first Gallagher Girl to sit in that sterile room – after all, debriefs *are* a part of the covert operations package. Still, I couldn't help squirming in the hard metal chair – maybe because it was cold in there, maybe because I was nervous, maybe because I was experiencing a slight underwear *situation*. (Note to self: develop a wedgie theory of interrogation – there could totally be something to it!) But the efficient-looking man in the wire-rim glasses was too busy twisting knobs and punching keys, trying to figure out what the truth sounded like coming from me, to care about my fidgeting.

"The Gallagher Academy doesn't teach interrogation procedures until we're juniors, you know?" I said, but the man just muttered, "Uh-huh."

"And I'm just a sophomore, so you shouldn't worry about the results coming out all screwy or anything. I'm not immune to your powers of interrogation." *Yet.*

"Good to know," he mumbled, but his eyes never left the screens.

"I know it's just standard protocol, so just…ask away." I was babbling, but couldn't seem to stop. "Really," I said. "Whatever you need to know, just—"

"Do you attend the Gallagher Academy for Exceptional Young Women?" the man blurted, and for reasons I will never understand I said, "Uh…yes?" as if it might be a trick question.

"Have you ever studied the subject of Covert Operations?"

"Yes," I said again, feeling my confidence, or maybe just my training, coming back to me.

"Did your Covert Operations coursework ever take you to the town of Roseville, Virginia?"

Even in that sterile room beneath Washington, D.C., I could almost feel the hot, humid night last September. I could almost hear the band and smell the corn dogs.

My stomach growled as I said, "Yes."

Polygraph Guy made notes and studied the bank of monitors that surrounded him. "Is that when you first noticed The Subject?"

Here's the thing about being a spy in love: your boyfriend never has a name. People like Polygraph Guy were never just going to call him Josh. He would always be The Subject, a *person of interest*. Taking away his name was their way of taking him away, or what was left of him. So I said, "Yes," and tried not to let my voice crack.

"And you utilised your training to develop a relationship with The Subject?"

"Gee, when you say it like that—"

"Yes or no, Ms—"

"Yes!"

Which, I would like to point out, is not nearly as bad as it sounds since, for example, you don't need a search warrant to go through someone's rubbish. Seriously. Once it hits the kerb it is totally fair game – you can look it up.

But somehow I knew that the Office of Operative

Development and Human Intelligence was probably far less concerned about the rubbish thing than it was about what came *after* the rubbish thing. So I was fully prepared when Polygraph Guy said, "Did The Subject follow you during your Covert Operations final examination?"

I thought about Josh appearing in the abandoned warehouse during finals week, bursting through walls and commandeering a forklift to "save" me, so I swallowed hard as I said, "Yes."

"And was The Subject given memory-modification tea to erase the events of that night?"

It sounded so easy coming from him, so black-and-white. Sure, my mom gave Josh some tea that's supposed to wipe a person's memory blank, erase a few hours of their life, and give everyone a clean slate. But clean slates are a rare thing in any life – especially a spy's life – so I didn't let myself wonder for the millionth time what Josh remembered about that night, about me. I didn't torture myself with any of the questions that might never have answers as I sat there, knowing that there is no such thing as black-and-white – remembering that my whole life is, by definition, a little bit grey.

I nodded, then muttered, "Yes." Like it or not, I knew I had to say the word out loud.

He made some more notes, punched some keys. "Are you currently involved with The Subject in any way?"

"No," I blurted, because I knew that much was true.

I hadn't seen Josh, hadn't spoken to him, hadn't even hacked into his e-mail account over the winter holidays, which, given present circumstances, turned out to be a pretty good thing. (Plus, I had spent the last two weeks in Nebraska with Grandpa and Grandma Morgan, and they have dial-up internet, which takes forever!)

Then the man in the wire-rim glasses looked away from the screen and straight into my eyes. "And do you intend to reinitiate contact with The Subject despite strict rules prohibiting such a relationship?"

There it was: the question I'd pondered for weeks.

There I was: Cammie the Chameleon – the Gallagher Girl who had risked the most sacred sisterhood in the history of espionage. For a boy.

"Ms Morgan," Polygraph Guy said, growing impatient, "are you going to reinitiate contact with The Subject?"

"No," I said softly.

Then I glanced back at the screen to see if I was lying.

Chapter 2

If you've ever been debriefed by the CIA, then you probably know exactly how I felt two hours later as I sat in the backseat of a limousine, watching city give way to suburbs and suburbs to countryside. Dirty piles of blackened ice became thick blankets of lush white snow, and the world seemed clean and new – ready for a fresh start.

I was through with lying (except for official cover stories, of course). And sneaking around (well...except when involved in covert operations). I was going to be normal! (Or as normal as a student at spy school ever gets a chance to be.)

I was going to be...myself.

I looked at my mom and reiterated the promise that I would never let a boy come between me and my family or my friends or matters of national security ever again. Then I realised that she'd hardly said a word since we'd left Washington. "I did okay, didn't I?" I asked, almost afraid to hear the answer.

"Of course, sweetie. You aced it."

Which, not to sound conceited or anything, I kind of already knew, because A) I've always tested well, and B) people who fail polygraphs don't usually walk out of top-secret facilities and get driven back to spy school.

Then I thought about the one-way glass. "You got to watch, didn't you?" I asked, fully expecting her to say, "You were great, sweetie", or I think this might be worth some extra credit", or "Remember, breathing is key when you're being inter-rogated with a TruthMaster 3000". But no. She didn't say any of those things.

Instead, my mom just placed her hand over mine and said, "No, Cam. I'm afraid I had some things to do."

Things? My mom had missed my first official government interrogation because of...*things*?

I might have asked for details, begged her to explain how she could miss such a milestone in a young spy's life, but I know the things my mom does typically involve national security, fake passports, and the occasional batch of weapons-grade plutonium, so I said, "Oh. OK," knowing I shouldn't feel hurt, but feeling it anyway.

We sat in silence until there was nothing to see outside my window but the tall stone fences that circle the

17

Gallagher Academy grounds. Home.

I felt the limo slow and stop behind the long line of nearly identical chauffeured cars that brought us back to school each semester. It had been more than a century since Gillian Gallagher had decided to turn her family's mansion into an elite boarding school, and even then, after more than a hundred years of educating exceptional young women, no one in the town of Roseville, Virginia, had a clue just how exceptional we really were.

Not even my ex-boyfriend.

"*Tell me everything!*" someone cried as soon as I opened the limo door. Sunlight bounced off the snow, blinding me before I could focus on my best friend's face. Bex's caramel-coloured eyes bore into me, her brown skin glowed, and, as usual, she looked like an Egyptian goddess. "Was it awesome?"

She stepped aside as I crawled out of the car, but didn't pause because…well…Bex doesn't exactly have a *pause*. She has a *play* and a *fast-forward* and occasionally a *rewind*, but Rebecca Baxter didn't become the first non-American Gallagher Girl in history by standing still.

"Did they grill you?" she continued. Then her eyes went wide and her accent grew heavy. "Was there torture?"

Well, of course there wasn't torture; but before I could say so, Bex exclaimed, "I bet it was bloody brilliant!" Most little girls in England grow up wanting to marry a prince. Bex grew up wanting to kick James Bond's butt and assume his double-0 ranking.

My mom walked around the side of the car. "Good afternoon, Rebecca. I trust you made it back from the airport OK?" And then, despite the bright sun that glowed around us, a shadow seemed to cross my best friend's face.

"Yes, ma'am." She pulled one of my bags from the open boot. "Thanks again for letting me spend the winter holidays with you." Most people wouldn't have noticed the slight change in her voice, the faint vulnerability of her smile. But I understand what it's like not to know what continent your parents are on, or when you'll see them again. If ever. My mom was standing right beside me, but all Bex had was a coded message saying her parents were representing England's MI6 in a joint project with the CIA, and that, like it or not, they couldn't exactly come home for Christmas.

When Mom hugged Bex and whispered, "You're always welcome with us, sweetheart," I couldn't help thinking about how Bex had both of her parents some of the time, and I had one of my parents most of the time, but right then, neither of us seemed entirely happy with the deal.

We stood in silence for a minute, watching my mom walk away. I could have asked Bex about her parents. She could have mentioned my dad. But instead I just turned to her and said, "I got to meet the woman who bugged the Berlin Embassy in 1962."

And that was all it took to make my best friend smile.

We started for the main doors, pushing through the crowded foyer and up the Grand Staircase. We were halfway to our rooms when someone...or rather, something...stopped us in our tracks.

"Ladies," Patricia Buckingham called as I reached for the door to the East Wing – and the fastest route to our rooms. I tried the knob, but it wouldn't budge.

"It's..." I twisted harder, "...stuck!"

"It's not stuck, ladies," Buckingham called again, her genteel British accent carrying above the noise in the foyer below. "It's locked," she said, as if we have locked doors all the time at the Gallagher Academy, which, let me tell you – we don't. I mean, sure, a lot of our doors are protected by National Security Agency-approved codes or retinal scanners, but they're never just...locked. (Because, really, what's the point when there are entire sections of our library labelled *Locks: The Manipulation and Disabling of*.)

"I'm afraid the security department spent the winter holidays fixing a series of, shall we say, *gaps* in the security system." Professor Buckingham eyed me over the top of her reading glasses, and I felt a guilty lump settle in my gut. "And they discovered that the wing had been contaminated with fumes from the chemistry labs.

Therefore, this corridor is off-limits for the time being; you're going to have to find another way to your rooms."

Well, after three and a half years of exploring every inch of the Gallagher mansion, I knew better than anyone that there *are* other ways to our rooms (some of which require closed-toe shoes, a Phillips-head screwdriver, and fifty yards of rappel-a-cord). But before I could mention any of them, Buckingham turned back to us and said, "Oh, and Cameron, dear, please make sure your alternate route doesn't involve crawling inside any walls."

This whole fresh-start thing was going to be harder than I thought.

Bex and I started towards the back stairs, where Courtney Bauer was modelling the boots she'd got for Hanukkah. When we passed the sophomore common room we saw Kim Lee showing off the derivation of the Proadsky Position she'd mastered during the holidays. We saw girls of every size, shape, and colour, and I felt more and more at home with every step. Finally, I pushed open the door to our room and was halfway through the throw-your-suitcase-onto-the-bed manoeuvre when someone grabbed me from behind.

"Oh my gosh!" Liz cried. "I've been so worried!"

My suitcase landed hard on my foot, but I couldn't really cry out in pain because Liz was still squeezing, and even though she weighs less than a hundred pounds, Liz can squeeze pretty hard when she wants to.

"Bex said you had to go in for questioning," Liz said. "She said it was *Top Secret!*"

Yeah. Pretty much everything we do is *Top Secret*, but the novelty has never worn off for Liz, probably because, unlike Bex and me and seventy per cent of our classmates, Liz's parents drive Volvos and serve on school committees and have never had to kill a man with a copy of *Hello* magazine. (Not that anyone can prove my mom actually did that – it's totally just a rumour.)

"Liz, it's okay," I said, pulling free. "It was just a debrief. It was normal protocol stuff."

"So…" Liz started. "You aren't in trouble?" She picked up a massive book. "Because article nine, section seven of the *Handbook of Operative Development* clearly states that operatives in training may be placed on temporary—"

"Liz," Bex said, cutting her off, "please tell me you didn't spend the morning memorising that book."

"I didn't memorise it," Liz said defensively. "I just…read it." Which, when you have a photographic memory, is pretty much the same thing, but I didn't say so.

Down the hall, I heard Eva Alvarez explaining how Buenos Aires on New Year's Eve is awesome. A pair of freshmen rushed by our door talking about who would make a better Gallagher Girl: Buffy the Vampire Slayer or Veronica Mars (a debate made much more interesting by the fact it was taking place in Farsi).

Bright sunlight shone through our window, bouncing

off the snow. It was a new semester and my best friends were beside me. All seemed right with the world.

Thirty minutes later I was in my uniform, making my way down the spiral staircase, towards the Grand Hall with the rest of the students. Well, *most* of the students.

"Where's Macey?"

"Oh, she's back already," Liz said, but I knew that much. After all, it was kind of hard to miss Macey's wardrobe full of designer clothes, her stash of ridiculously expensive skin care products (many of which are legal only in Europe), and the fact that someone had very recently been sleeping in her bed.

The last time I'd seen our fourth roommate, she'd been preparing for three weeks in the Swiss Alps with her senator father, her cosmetics-heiress mom, and a celebrity chef from the Food Channel; but Macey McHenry had come back early. And now she was nowhere to be seen.

Bex was looking around, too, staring over the heads of the seventh graders walking in front of us. "She said she had a bit of research to do in the library, but that was hours ago. I thought she'd meet us down here, but..." she trailed off, still looking.

"You guys go eat," I said, stepping away from the crowd and starting down the hall. "I'll find her."

I pulled open the heavy library doors and stepped inside the massive bookshelf-lined room. Comfy leather sofas and old oak tables surrounded a roaring fire. And there, in the centre of it all, was Macey McHenry. Her head was resting on the latest edition of *Molecular Chemistry Monthly*, pink highlighter marks were on her cheek, and a puddle of drool had run from her mouth onto the wooden desktop.

"Macey," I whispered, reaching out to gently shake her shoulder.

"What? Huh...Cammie?" She struggled upright and blinked at me. "What time is it?" she cried, jumping up and knocking a stack of flash cards to the floor.

I bent down to help her pick them up. "The welcome-back dinner is about to start."

"Great," she said, sounding like someone who didn't think it was great at all.

Her glossy black hair stuck out at odd angles, and her normally bright blue eyes were dazed with sleep. Even though I knew better, I couldn't help but say, "So, did you have a nice holiday?"

She cut me a look that could kill (and will – just as soon as our head scientist, Dr Fibs, perfects his looks-can-kill technology).

"Sure." Macey blew a stray piece of hair away from her beautiful face and pulled the last of the flash cards into a pile. "Right up until my parents saw my marks."

"But you got great marks! You covered nearly two semesters' worth of work. You—"

"Got four A's and three B's," Macey finished for me.

24

"*I* know!" I cried. After all, I had personally tutored Macey in the finer points of macroeconomics, molecular regeneration, and conversational Swahili.

"And according to *the Senator*," Macey said, keeping up her unspoken vow never to call her father by name, "there's no way *I* am capable of earning four A's and three B's, so therefore I must be cheating."

"But…" I struggled to find the words. "But… Gallagher Girls don't cheat!" And it's true. Not to sound dramatic or anything, but a Gallagher Girl's real marks don't come in pass or fail – they're measured in life or death. But Senator McHenry didn't know that. I looked at the gorgeous debutante who had been kicked out of every prep academy on the East Coast and was now earning A's and B's at spy school, and I realised the senator didn't know a lot of things. Not even his own daughter.

The library was empty around us, but I still lowered my voice as I said, "Macey, you should tell my mom. She could call your dad. We could—"

"No way!" Macey said, as if I never let her have any fun. "Besides, I already know what I'm going to do."

We'd reached the heavy doors of the library, but I paused for the answer. "What?"

"Study." Macey cocked a perfectly plucked eyebrow. "Next time I'll get *all* A's." And then she smiled as if, after sixteen years of practice, she'd finally found the ultimate way to defy her parents.

I heard voices in the corridor outside, which was strange because at that moment the entire Gallagher Academy student population was waiting in the Grand Hall. Something made us freeze. And wait. And despite the heavy doors between us, I could clearly hear my mom say, "No, Cammie doesn't know anything."

Well, as a spy (not to mention a girl), there are many, many sentences that will make me stop and listen, and, needless to say, "Cammie doesn't know anything" is totally one of them!

I leaned closer to the door while, beside me, Macey's big blue eyes got even wider. She leaned in and whispered, "*What* don't you know?"

"She didn't suspect anything?" Mr Solomon, my dreamy CoveOps instructor, asked.

"*What* didn't you suspect?" asked Macey.

Well, of course the whole point of not knowing and not suspecting is that I neither *knew* nor *suspected*, but I couldn't point that out because, at the moment, my mom was on the opposite side of the door saying, "No, she was being debriefed at the time."

I thought back to the long, quiet ride from Washington, the way my mom had stared at the frosty countryside as she'd told me that she hadn't watched my interrogation – that she'd had *things* to do.

"We can't tell her, Joe," Mom said. "We can't tell anyone. Not until we have to."

"Not about black thorn?"

"Not about anything." And then Mom sighed. "I just want things to stay as normal as possible for as long as possible."

I looked at Macey. Normal had just taken on a whole new meaning.

After they left, Macey and I slipped back to the Grand Hall and the sophomore table. Mom had already taken her place at the front of the room. I know that Liz whispered, "What took you so long?" as we sat down. But beyond that, I wasn't sure of anything, because, to tell you the truth, I was having a little trouble hearing. And talking. And walking.

All moms have secrets – mine more than most – and even though I've always known that there are lots of things my mom can never tell me, it had never occurred to me that there were things she might be *keeping from* me. It may not sound like a big difference, but it is.

Mom gripped the podium in front of her and looked out at the hundred girls who sat ready for a new semester. "Welcome back, everyone. I hope you had a wonderful winter holiday," she said.

"Cammie," Bex whispered, eyeing me and then Macey. "Something's going on with you two. Isn't it?"

Before I could answer, my mom continued, "I'd like to begin with the very exciting news that this semester we will be offering a new course, History of Espionage, taught by Professor Buckingham." Light applause filled the Grand Hall as our most senior staff member gave a small wave.

"And also," my mom said slowly, "as many of you have no doubt noticed, the East Wing will be off-limits for the time being, since recent work to the mansion revealed that it has been contaminated by fumes from the chemistry labs."

"Cammie," Liz said, scooting closer, "you look kind of…pukey."

Well I *felt* kind of pukey.

"And most of all," my mom said, "I want to wish everyone a great semester."

The silence that had filled the hall a moment before evaporated into a chorus of talking girls and passing plates. I tried to turn the volume down, to listen to the thoughts that swirled inside my mind like the snow that blew outside. I closed my eyes tightly, forcing the room to dissolve away, until suddenly, everything became clear.

And I whispered the fact that I'd known for years but only just remembered.

"There is no ventilation access from the chem labs to the East Wing."

Chapter 3

There are many pros and cons to living in a two-hundred-year-old mansion. For example: having about a dozen highly secluded places where you can sit and discuss classified information: PRO.

The fact that none of these places are well heated and/or insulated when you are discussing said information in the middle of the winter: CON.

Two hours after our welcome-back dinner, Macey was leaning against the stone wall at the top of one of the mansion's tallest towers, drawing her initials on the win-dow's frosty panes. Liz paced, Bex shivered, and I sat on the floor with my arms around my knees, too tired to get my blood flowing despite the chill that had seeped through my uniform and settled in my bones.

"So that's it, then?" Bex asked. "That's everything

your mom and Mr Solomon said? Verbatim?"

Macey and I looked at each other, recalling the conversation we'd overheard and the story we'd just told. Then we both nodded and said, "Verbatim."

At that moment, the entire sophomore class was probably enjoying our last homework-free night for a very long time (rumour had it Tina Walters was organising a Jason Bourne-athon), but the four of us stayed in that tower room, freezing our you-know-whats off, listening for the creaking hinges of the heavy oak door at the base of the stairs that would warn us if we were no longer alone.

"I can't believe it," Liz said as she continued to walk back and forth – maybe to keep warm, but probably because…well…Liz has always been a pacer. (And we've got the worn spots on our bedroom floor to prove it.)

"Cam," Liz asked, "are you *sure* the East Wing couldn't have been contaminated by fumes from the chem labs?"

"Of course she's sure," Bex said with a sigh.

"But are you absolutely, positively, one hundred per cent sure?" Liz asked again. After all, as the youngest person ever published in *Scientific American*, Liz kind of likes things verified, cross-referenced, and proven beyond a shadow of a doubt.

"Cam," Bex said, turning to me, "how many ventilation shafts are there in the kitchen?"

"Fourteen – unless you're counting the pantry. Are

30

you counting the pantry?" I asked, which must have been enough to prove my expertise, because Macey rolled her eyes and sank to the floor beside me. "She's sure."

In the dim light of the cold room I could see snowflakes swirl in the wind outside, blowing from the mansion's roof (or...well...the parts of the roof that aren't protected with electrified security shingles). But inside, the four of us were quiet and still.

"Why would they lie?" Liz asked, but Bex, Macey, and I just looked at her, none of us really wanting to point out the obvious: *Because they're spies.*

It's something Bex and I had understood all our lives. Judging by the look on her face, Macey had caught on, too (after all, her dad *is* in politics). But Liz hadn't grown up knowing that lies aren't just the things we tell – they're the lives we lead. Liz still wanted to believe that parents and teachers always tell the truth, that if you eat your vegetables and brush your teeth, nothing bad will ever happen. I'd known better for a long time, but Liz still had a little naïveté left. I, for one, hated to see her lose it.

"What's black thorn?" Macey asked, looking at each of us in turn. "I mean, you guys don't know either, right? It's not just a me-being-the-new-girl thing?"

Everyone shook their heads, then looked to me. "Never heard of it," I said.

And I hadn't. It wasn't the name of any covert operation we'd ever analysed, any scientific breakthrough we'd ever studied. Black thorn or Blackthorne or whatever could have been anyone, anything, anywhere! And whoever…or whatever…or wherever it was, it had made my mom miss some quality mom-daughter interrogation time. It had also forced my Covert Operations instructor to hold a clandestine conversation with my headmistress. It had crept inside the Gallagher Academy for Exceptional Young Women (or at least its East Wing), and so there we were, not quite sure what a Gallagher Girl was supposed to do now.

I mean, we had three perfectly viable options: 1) We could forget what we'd heard and go to bed. 2) We could embrace the whole "honesty" thing and tell my mom all we knew. Or 3) I could be…myself. Or, more specifically, the me I *used* to be.

"The forbidden hall of the East Wing is almost directly beneath us," I began slowly. "All we have to do is access the dumbwaiter shaft on the fourth floor, manoeuvre through the heating vents by the Culture and Assimilation classroom, and rappel fifty or so feet through the ductwork." But even as I said it, I knew it couldn't be nearly as easy as it sounded.

"So…" Macey said, "what are we waiting for?" She jumped to her feet and started for the door.

"Macey! Wait!" Everyone looked at me. "The security department did a lot of work over the holiday." I pulled my legs closer, wrapped my arms tighter. "I don't know what kind of upgrades they made, what they might have changed. They were all over those tunnels and passageways, and…" I trailed off, grateful that Bex was there to finish for me.

"We don't know what's in there, Macey," she said, even though the fact that we didn't know what lay waiting in the East Wing was kind of the point, and I could tell by the look on her face that Macey was getting ready to say so.

"Surprises," I finished slowly, "as a rule…are bad."

Macey sank to the floor beside me while I told myself that everything I'd said was true. After all, it was a risky operation. We didn't have adequate intel or nearly enough time to prep. I can list a dozen perfectly logical reasons why I stayed on that stone floor, but the one I didn't tell my friends was that I had promised my mom that my days of sneaking around and breaking rules were over. And I'd kind of hoped my vow would last longer than twenty-four hours.

"So, what do we do now?" Liz asked.

Bex smiled. "Oh," she said mischievously, "we'll think of something."

Covert Operations Report
Summary of Surveillance
By Cameron Morgan, Rebecca Baxter, Elizabeth Sutton, and Macey McHenry (hereafter referred to as "The Operatives")

33

When faced with the knowledge that faculty members of the Gallagher Academy for Exceptional Young Women were planning a rogue operation, The Operatives began a research and recognisance mission to determine the following:

1. What was such a big freaking deal that no one wanted The Operatives to know about it?
2. Why were The Operatives no longer allowed in the East Wing? (A change that had added ten and a half minutes to their average daily commute between classes!)
3. Who or what was Black Thorn? Or maybe Blackthorne? (Is it possible that Headmistress Morgan and Mr Solomon were taking on a group of terrorists-slash-florists?)
4. What does Mr Solomon look like with his shirt off? (Because, if you're going to set up an observation post, you may as well be thorough.)

When I woke up the next morning I tried not to think about the night before, but it's kind of hard to forget covert and potentially dangerous missions when A) The dirty tower floor left a stain on your best school skirt. B) At breakfast, your mom says, "Good morning, Cam. Did you girls have fun last night?" which everyone knows translates to *I'm acting perfectly normal because I totally have something to hide.* And C) Avoiding the mysteriously off-limits East Wing means you have to find alternate routes to sixty per cent of your daily destinations.

On my way downstairs I walked slowly past the door that opened into the East Wing. It was just another door – dark, solid wood, an old brass knob. There were hundreds of doors like it in the mansion, but this one was forbidden, so like any good spy, I wanted to open that one.

I felt Kim Lee fall into step beside me as she glanced at the door and said, "Going around is such a pain." Of course she didn't think about the fact that half of our teachers could have been behind that very door at this very moment, planning an attack on some rogue florists!

I, of course, was having trouble thinking about anything else.

Not even the sight of Mr Smith appearing in Countries of the World (COW) with a jar of coins, telling us to make change for a dollar in eight different currencies while factoring in exchange rates, could make me stop obsessing about that door and the secrets it was masking.

Even Madame Dabney's lecture on the art of perfect thank-you notes and their obviously underutilised coded message potential couldn't pull my mind away from the East Wing.

We already had two hours' worth of homework and the promise of a pop quiz on the poisonous plants of Southeast Asia; all the teachers were acting like they either had no idea what was going on, or had sworn to take the secret to their graves (which could have been true, actually).

It was business as usual at the Gallagher Academy, and as we started downstairs after Culture and Assimilation (C&A), it almost felt like the holiday had never happened.

Almost.

"Well, this is it," Liz said. Bex and I started for the elevator that was concealed in the narrow hallway beneath the Grand Staircase.

"What is it?" I asked. Then I turned and saw that Liz wasn't following us to our next class.

Instead, she hooked her thumbs in the straps of her backpack and took a step away. "I've got Advanced Organic Chemistry."

But Bex and I didn't have Advanced Organic Chemistry. Bex and I had Covert Operations. From that moment on, the two of us were going to be training for a life of missions and fieldwork while Liz prepared for a career in a lab or an office. I thought about the forms we'd filled out last semester, the choice I'd made to walk away from any hope of a safe, normal life – from boys like Josh. So it wasn't any wonder that my voice cracked when I said, "Oh. OK."

Bex and I stared into the mirror that hid the elevator's entrance, then waited for the red beam to scan our retinal images and clear us for our second semester in Sublevel One. I tried not to think about how, for the first time since seventh grade, Liz wouldn't be beside us.

Bex must have been thinking the same thing, because pretty soon she said, "Are you *sure* you want to spend the next two and a half years doing experiments and cracking codes?" A wicked twinkle appeared in her eye as she studied Liz's pale reflection. "Because the CoveOps class is gonna do underwater exercises eventually, and you know Mr Solomon will have to take his shirt off."

A portrait of Gillian Gallagher hung on the wall behind us; I saw her eyes flash green, then the mirror slid aside, revealing the small elevator to the Covert Operations classroom. Liz watched the doors slide closed behind us, then Bex turned around and yelled, "But Mr Mosckowitz might go topless sometime, too!"

And then I heard Liz laugh.

"She'll be okay without us, right?" Bex asked.

We heard the clanking of a suit of armour falling to the floor and Liz's distinctive "Oopsy daisy."

As the elevator started to move, Bex said, "Don't answer that."

Here's the thing you need to know about Sublevel One: It's big. Like, I've-seen-football-stadiums-that-are-smaller big. And while the rest of the mansion is made of old stone and ancient wood, there's nothing about the frosted-glass partitions and stainless steel furniture of the Covert Operations classroom that could ever be confused with a two-hundred-year-old mansion that houses privileged girls.

Bex and I stepped off the elevator, our footsteps echoing as we passed the CoveOps library, full of books so sensitive you can never ever take them out of the Subs. (They're made out of paper that will disintegrate if it's ever exposed to natural light, just to be on the safe side.) We passed big burly guys from the maintenance department, who smiled and said, "Knock 'em dead, girls." (Knowing the guys from *our* maintenance department, they may very well have meant it literally.)

I slid into my chair, trying not to think about Liz or *the door* or anything other than the fact that I was finally back in the one part of the Gallagher Academy that never pretended to be anything other than what it is.

That was before Tina Walters leaned towards me, grinning and snapping her gum as only a third-generation spy-slash-gossip-columnist's daughter can do. "So, Cammie, is it true they sent a SWAT team to drag you out of your grandparents' house on Christmas morning?" Tina didn't wait for a response. "Because I heard you put up a good fight, but that they eventually pulled your Christmas stocking over your head and rolled you up in the tree skirt."

There will probably come a day when national security will rest in the hands of Tina Walters. Luckily, that wasn't the day.

"I was with her, Tina," Bex said. "Do you honestly think they could have taken both of us?"

Tina nodded, conceding the point. Before she could dig further, a deep voice said, "Static surveillance." Mr Solomon came strolling into class without so much as a hello. "It is the root of what we do, and it has one golden rule – name it!"

And then, despite everything, I half expected to see Liz's thin arm shoot into the air, but of course it was a different voice that answered. "The first rule of static surveillance is that the operative must use the simplest, least-intrusive means possible."

Well, my first thought was that Sublevel One had become contaminated with some kind of hallucinogenic chemical, because the girl who spoke *sounded* like Anna Fetterman. She *looked* like Anna Fetterman. But there was no way Anna Fetterman belonged on the Covert Operations track of study!

Don't get me wrong, I love Anna. Really, I do. But I once saw her give herself a bloody nose while opening a can of Pringles. (I'm soooo not even making that up.) And that's not the kind of thing that usually screams *Let me parachute onto the roof of a foreign embassy to bug the ambassador's cuff links*, if you know what I mean.

But did Mr Solomon act shocked? No, he just said, "Very good, Ms Fetterman," as if everything were perfectly normal – which…hello…it wasn't. I mean, Anna was taking CoveOps, my mom was hiding something from me, and there was an entire section of our school that even *I* couldn't access! Everything was not perfectly normal!

Joe Solomon had been an undercover operative for eighteen years, so naturally he was completely calm as he relaxed against his desk and said, "We deal in information, ladies. It's not about operations – it's about intelligence. It's not about cool gadgets – it's about getting the job done." Mr Solomon looked around the room. "In other words, don't bother to plant cameras in the living room if your target never shuts the blinds."

I started writing everything down, but then Mr Solomon slid Eva Alvarez's notebook off her desk and into her open bag. "No notes, ladies."

No notes? What did he mean no notes? Was he serious? (By the way, it was probably a good thing Liz wasn't on the CoveOps track, because her head would have been exploding about then!)

At the front of the room, Joe Solomon turned to the board and started diagramming a typical static surveillance scenario. Anna was gripping her pen so hard it looked like she was about to pull a muscle, but Mr Solomon must have that whole eyes-in-the-back-of-his-head thing, because he said, "I said no notes, Ms Fetterman," and Anna jerked away from her pen as if it had shocked her. (It might have – we do have some very specialised writing instruments here at the Gallagher Academy.)

"This is not a required course, ladies. You no longer have to be here." Mr Solomon turned around. His green eyes bore into us, and at that moment Joe Solomon wasn't just our hottest teacher, he was also our scariest. "Six of your classmates have already chosen a relatively safe life on the research and operations track of study. If you can't remember a fifty-minute lecture, then I'd encourage you to join them."

He turned back to the board and continued writing. "Your memory is your first and best weapon, ladies. Learn to use it."

I sat there for a long time, absorbing what he'd said, what it meant, knowing that he was right. Our memories are the only weapons we take with us no matter where we go, but then I thought about the second part of his statement – *Don't make things harder than they have to be.* I thought about what I'd overheard the night before. The look in my mom's eyes on the long, quiet ride home. And finally…Josh. And then I realised that my life would be a whole lot *easier* if there were some things I could forget.

☠

4

Summary of Surveillance

By utilising the "least-intrusive means possible"
model of covert operations, The Operatives were
able to ascertain the following:

According to some very popular Internet search
engines, "black thorn" is a common type of rose
fungus, but does not appear to be a code name for
any rogue government conspiracy theories.

There are approximately 1,947 people in the
United States named Blackthorne, but, according to
the tax office, none of them have listed their
profession as Spy, Spook, Ghoul, Assassin, Hitter,
Pro, Freelancer, Black Bag Man (or woman),
Operative, Agent, or Pavement Artist.

Seeing through the door to the East Wing wasn't

possible, because, despite rumours to the contrary, Dr Fibs's X-ray vision goggles had not passed beyond the prototype phase. (Which also explained why he was wearing that eye patch.)

A good thing about going to spy school is that you have genius friends with incredible abilities who are able to help you with any "special projects" that may come up. The bad part is that they really get into those "projects". Way into them.

"It's got to be in here somewhere!" Liz cried over the sound of heavy books crashing onto hard wood as she dropped volumes nine through fourteen of *Surveillance Through the Centuries* onto the library table.

I looked around the quiet room, waiting for someone to shush her, but all I heard was the crackling of wood in the fireplace and the sigh of a girl who, after spending every spare moment for a week barricaded in the library, was starting to lose faith in books. (And Liz is the girl who actually slept with a copy of *Advanced Encryption and You* during finals week of our eighth grade year!)

Macey tossed aside *The Chronicles of Chemical Warfare* that lay on her lap. "Maybe it's not *in* the library," Macey said, and I seriously thought Liz was going to hyperventilate or something. She might have if Macey hadn't crossed her legs and asked, "So what does that *mean*?"

Oh my gosh! I can't believe we hadn't asked that

question before – that somehow we'd forgotten one of the basic rules of covert operations: *everything* means *something*! Not finding something significant was maybe the most significant thing of all.

"Do you know how current something has to be not to be in these books?" Liz asked, backing away, sounding slightly terrified and a little bit giddy. She looked at the volumes on the table as if they were so dangerous they might explode (which is silly, since everyone knows the so-top-secret-they'll-explode-if-you-read-them-without-clearance books are stored in Sublevel Three).

"So Blackthorne must be—" Macey started, looking at me.

"Classified," I finished. "Really classified."

Spies keep secrets – it's what we do. So we sat in silence while the fire crackled and the truth washed over us: If Blackthorne was that Top Secret, then I was sure we'd never find it.

"You know, Cam," Bex said, smiling a smile that might be alarming on an ordinary girl, but on a girl with Bex's special talents it's downright terrifying, "there is *one place* we haven't looked." She tapped a finger against her chin in a gesture that, even for Bex, was especially dramatic. "Now, who do we know who has access to the headmistress's office?"

"No, Bex." I sat up straight and began stacking and restacking books. "No. No. No. I cannot spy on my mom!"

"Why not?" Bex asked as if I'd just told her I couldn't pull off wearing red lipstick (which, by the way, I can't).

"Because...*she's my mom*," I said, not even trying to hide the *duh* in my voice. "And she's one of the CIA's very best operatives. And...she's my mom!"

"Exactly! She would never suspect" – Bex paused for effect – "her own daughter." And then Bex, Liz, and Macey looked at me as if this were the best plan ever. Which it wasn't. At all. I mean, I know a little something about plans, having helped my father design a Trojan horse-type scenario to infiltrate a former Soviet nuclear missile silo that had been taken over by terrorists when I was seven. And *this* was not a good plan!

"Bex!" I cried. "I don't want to do this. It—"

But before I could finish, the library door swung open and I heard Macey say, "Hello, Ms Morgan."

Even though I'd been sitting relatively still for forty-five minutes, my heart felt like I'd just run a mile. Mom looked down at the Portuguese translation of *101 Classic Covers and the Spies Who've Used Them* and said, "What are you girls doing in the library on a sunny day like this?"

"COW extra credit," we all said, citing the cover story we'd agreed on before we left the room.

But still, my pulse didn't slow down. I just sat there, reminding myself that we weren't breaking any rules. I hadn't really told any lies. (Mr Smith *had* assigned extra credit, after all.) Technically, I hadn't broken my promise. Yet.

"OK," Mom said, smiling. "I'll see you tonight, Cam."

I felt Bex's eyes on me and knew what she was thinking – that I was going to be spending the evening with my mom. In her office. What kind of operative would I be if I didn't take advantage of the situation?

But then I thought about my mom and wondered what kind of daughter I would be if I did.

THINGS I'VE DONE
THAT I'M NOT NECESSARILY PROUD OF:
A list by Cameron Morgan

- One time I accidentally spilled all of Bex's detangling conditioner and refilled the bottle with volumising conditioner, and her hair got really big for a few weeks, but I never told her why.

- I once wore Liz's favourite yoga leggings without permission and totally stretched them out. Also, her favourite sweater.

- Whenever I'm in Nebraska I always pretend I'm too weak to open pickle jars, because Grandpa Morgan likes to do it for me.

- As I have thoroughly documented elsewhere, I once had a clandestine relationship with a really cute, really sweet boy and then lied about it. A lot.

- On the first Sunday after the winter holidays in my sophomore year, I helped Liz implant a camera in the watch Grandma gave me for my birthday. And then I wore it to Sunday-night supper in my mom's office so that I could do the worst thing I've ever done. Ever.

When you're the daughter of two secret agents, you learn pretty early that spies walk a moral tightrope. We do bad things for good reasons, and for the most part we can live with that. But that Sunday night, when I sat in my mom's office eating microwavable crab puffs and fingering my new custom-made spy watch, I thought about my cover: hungry daughter bonding with her mom-slash-mentor. Then I thought about my mission: do a basic recon of the headmistress's office and hope there will be a report titled *Operation Black Thorn* or *Contents of the East Wing* just lying around.

    Sunday-night supper in my mom's office is something I've been doing ever since Mom and I came to the Gallagher Academy. Usually, however, I don't feel nauseous until *after* I've eaten (because even though Mom once manufactured an antidote for a rare poison by using the contents of a hotel minibar, she has yet to master microwaves and hot plates).

"So," Mom said, gesturing to the small silver tray of puffs, "how are they?"

(Note to self: research bioweapon potential of microwavable crab puffs.)

"They're great!" I lied, and my mom smiled. No, scratch that – she glowed. And at that moment I seriously wanted to back out, to put the watch in my pocket and forget how I'd already memorised the exact position of everything on her desk in case I got a chance to snoop and then had to put things back. I wanted to stop being a spy and start being a daughter. Especially when Mom glanced at my wrist and said, "You're wearing Grandma's watch."

I rubbed my thumb over the smooth glass that now doubled as a telephoto lens. "Yeah."

"That's nice," she said, and smiled happily. Even though she seemed to be fine now, I thought about the worried woman I'd shared a limo with from Washington, and the conversation I'd overheard. I wasn't the only operative in that room clinging to her legend.

And then, before I could stop to think, I blurted, "Do you have any fingernail clippers?" Mom looked at me for a second, and I knew I couldn't back out now, so I held out my right hand, which thankfully, wasn't shaking. "I've got a hangnail that's driving me crazy."

"Sure, sweetie," Mom said. "In my desk. Top drawer."

So see, I didn't even have to pick the lock or fake the fingerprint-activated drawers. I was perfectly within my daughterly rights as I moved to my mom's desk and rummaged around for the clippers.

A brief search of the headmistress's desk revealed the following:

Headmistress Morgan had ten different lipsticks in her desk (only three of which were for purely cosmetic uses).

Mom carried a small pan into her private bathroom and turned on the water, and that's when I took pictures of every single thing in her rubbish bin.

Headmistress Morgan had, evidently, been fighting off a cold, because her rubbish contained fourteen used tissues and an empty bottle of Vitamin C.

I knocked a paper clip dispenser off her desk and channelled Liz with a loud "Oopsy daisy." Then I huddled on the floor as I picked up paper clips with one hand and rifled through her bottom desk drawers with the other.

Of all the items the Gallagher Academy receives royalty revenues from, elastoplasts are surprisingly the most profitable.

*

I could hear my mom on the far side of the room, stirring things, pouring things. "Did you find them?" she called out.

I held up the nail clippers with one hand while I closed her bottom drawer with the other.

I smiled and waved my manicured fingers and thought, I am a terrible daughter.

But my mom only smiled in return, because maybe I'm also a pretty good spy.

Ironically, the one person who could explain the difference was the one person I totally couldn't ask.

I placed the nail clippers back where I'd found them and looked down at a desk that even an expert would swear had never been touched. I placed my palms against the middle drawer and felt my fingertips brush against the smooth wood of the underside, the cool metal track on which it ran. But something else, too. Something thin and worn.

"I know this semester is going to be a big adjustment for you, kiddo," Mom said. She stirred a bubbling concoction in a slow cooker while I pressed a finger against the paper – felt it move.

"And last semester. Well, I can only imagine what it must have been like – the reports, the debriefings."

I probably hadn't found anything important; after all, the underside of a drawer isn't a preferred hiding place for a spy – nothing about it is secure or protected. But it is a good hiding place for a woman – a place to keep something you want nearby but out of sight.

"And I want you to know," Mom went on, "that I am so proud of you."

Yes, that's right, not only was I invading my mom's personal space right under her nose, but that's the moment she chose to tell me how proud she was of my new-and-improved behaviour! It was official: I was a terrible person.

Then I felt the paper give. It fluttered through the air and landed right on my lap. And from that point on I barely heard a word my mom said.

Dad. It was a picture of Dad – but like no picture I'd ever seen, because for starters, he looked older than he did in the pictures Grandma had given me, and younger than he did in the pictures of him and my mom. And in this picture, my father wasn't alone.

Mr Solomon's arm was around my father's shoulders. They stood on a baseball field. They were young. They were strong. And if I hadn't known better, I would have sworn they were both immortal.

But I did know better. And that, I guess, was the problem.

"Did you find what you needed, sweetheart?" Mom asked, and I thought it was a really good question. I aimed my watch at the photo, imagined the faint click as I took a picture. "Cam," Mom said again, moving towards me.

"I'm not feeling too well," I said, and slipped the picture back to where my mom kept it hidden. From me.

From herself. From whoever. I moved away from the desk, towards the door. "Can we maybe do supper another time?"

"Cam," Mom said, stopping me. She put her hand against my forehead like Grandma Morgan always does. "It could be a cold – you know something has been going around." I did know. I'd already seen the proof in her rubbish bin.

"I think I just need to go to bed," I said. "It's pretty late."

But then I opened the door, and there, in the Hall of History, I saw Bex.

And Liz was sitting on her shoulders.

Chapter 5

Time's a strange thing at the Gallagher Academy. Usually it flies. But sometimes it gets really, really slow. Needless to say, this was one of *those* times.

The Operatives modified a Mobile Observation Device (aka Macey's new digital camera) and attached it to the bookcase across from the entrance to the headmistress's office with a Retractable Adhesion Unit (aka duct tape) and programmed it to take pictures at ninety-second intervals.

Down the corridor, I saw Macey kneeling in front of the mysteriously locked door to the East Wing.

The Operatives secured an Entry/Exit Detection

Device (aka a piece of string) to the doorknob in question, knowing it would fall off if the door was opened in The Operatives' absence.

For a split second, everything seemed to freeze, but then I heard my mom say, "What is it, Cam?" She walked towards me.

"Nothing." I closed the door and leaned against it. "It's just…" *It's just that my friends are completely insane and on the other side of this door right now, doing things that they really aren't supposed to be doing, and if you catch them you'll be really angry – or proud – but probably angry.*

"It's just…I wanted to tell you that I think I'm really in a good place this semester." (Because technically, at that moment, the best possible place was between the headmistress and my roommates.) "And I was thinking about what you said," I went on. "I'm committed to—"

But then a bang on the door cut me off, and I had a bad feeling that Liz had fallen from Bex's shoulders and knocked herself unconscious on the doorknob.

"Cam," Mom said, inching closer. "You gonna get that?"

But I didn't dare turn around. "Get what?" Another knock. *"Ooooh. Thaaaat."*

I opened the door. Please let it be Bex, I prayed. Or Liz… Or Macey… Or…

Anyone but Joe Solomon!

Oh my gosh! Could the night get any worse? Yes, it

54

turns out – it could. Because not only was one of the CIA's best secret agents standing in front of me, but my best friends in the world were twenty feet behind him, being secretive and agenty! (I know because I could see Macey's hand holding a compact mirror around the corner to see whether or not the coast was clear. Which, obviously, it wasn't!)

I had to buy some time – a minute, thirty seconds at least – so Bex, Liz, and Macey could pull themselves from their hiding places and get out of there.

So I said, "Oh, hello, Mr Solomon," because Madame Dabney has trained me to be socially gracious, and Mr Solomon himself has trained me to act normal under the most abnormal circumstances.

"Ms Morgan, I hate to bother you, but…" Mr Solomon looked past me towards my mom. "Those records you asked for, Rachel." He handed Mom a plain brown envelope.

An envelope bearing the word *Blackthorne* in Mr Solomon's careful writing.

And then time got really slow again.

"Cam?" Mom said behind me. "You really aren't feeling well, are you sweetie?"

"No," I muttered. I was staring at the first piece of concrete evidence that Blackthorne wasn't some weird dream I'd had, and yet I just stood there, looking at my Covert Operations instructor but seeing the man in the picture – my father's friend.

"OK, I'm going to go," I said with a glance at my mom. "And you guys have probably got...stuff...to do. And..."

I could have said a dozen things in a dozen languages, but before I could blurt a single one I heard a voice at the end of the Hall of History call, "There you are!"

And then the thing that I'd been fearing happened: Mr Solomon turned around.

But there's a difference between getting caught and allowing yourself to be found, and right then, Macey, Bex, and Liz were walking through the Hall of History, hiding in plain sight.

"We can't hold movie night forever, Cam," Bex said.

So I turned my back on my mom and Mr Solomon, and then, envelope or not, I walked away.

Do you know how many things I was feeling as we got to the room? A lot. *A lot.* For starters, there was the crab-puff thing. And then there was the envelope thing. But as soon as our door was closed and our stereo was on, I turned to my best friends and cried, "You planted surveillance equipment in the Hall of History while my mom was in her office!" because I guess that was the thing I felt the loudest.

"Oh, Cam," Bex said, shrugging slightly. "It was just a little recon."

Deep down, all I really wanted to do was put on my comfy pyjamas and go to sleep and brush the crab-puff taste out of my mouth (but not necessarily in that order). But instead I snapped, "Yeah, well you almost got caught – you almost got *me* caught. And getting debriefed by the security department isn't as much fun as it sounds, guys." I forced a laugh. "Trust me."

I said it kind of snotty, but Bex didn't answer. She didn't even get mad. Instead, she looked at me as only a best friend-slash-spy-slash-person-who-has-been-trained-on-reading-body-language can do. She climbed onto her bed and crossed her long legs. "You found something."

I could have denied it. I could have lied. But right then I was in the one room in the mansion where I could never disappear.

"Actually, I did." I told them what I'd found in my mom's desk. I listed the contents of her rubbish – even the shades of her lipstick. And finally, I told them about the envelope.

"We've got to get it!" Bex exclaimed, sounding as excited as a kid on Christmas morning. "We can wait until everyone goes to bed and then break into the office."

"That's not a good idea, Bex," I said as I slipped on my pyjamas, took off my watch, and pulled my hair into an old stretched-out hairband.

"Come on, Cam," Bex pleaded, while Macey and Liz looked on. "If anyone can get into the headmistress's office, it's you!"

"No!" I snapped, maybe because I knew better than to

let Bex work up any momentum; maybe because I was still completely on edge. But maybe because sometimes a girl just really needs to snap at someone who she knows will forgive her later.

I started for the bathroom, but Bex was right behind me. "Why not?"

"Because it's not a game," I said, talking louder than I wanted, but somehow unable to lower my voice. "Because sometimes spies get caught. Because sometimes spies get hurt. Because sometimes—"

"We've got pictures!" Liz cried triumphantly. Thin wires ran from my new watch to her computer. Images flashed across the screen. Crab puffs. File folders. And finally...

Dad.

Because sometimes spies don't come home.

The picture I had taken filled the screen. My jeans were like a denim border – a frame behind the snapshot that had landed on my lap. Liz zoomed in. She magnified.

"Ooh," Macey said. "Who's the hottie?"

"That's Mr Solomon, Macey," I said, starting for the bathroom because, well, I didn't want to cry in front of my friends. And one of the advantages of the face-washing process is that you have an excuse for squinting your eyes and looking away.

"Not Mr Solomon," Macey said. "The other guy. Is he Blackthorne?"

"No, Macey," Bex said, saving me the trouble. I glanced in the bathroom mirror and saw Bex turn from the screen and catch my eye in the glass. "That's Cam's dad."

We study a lot of dangerous stuff at the Gallagher Academy, but there are some things so feared that they're never, ever mentioned. Everyone knows my dad was in the CIA. That he went on a mission and never came home. Now there's an empty grave in the family plot in Nebraska. Everyone knows, but no one ever asks to hear the story. And that night, Macey was no different.

I splashed cold water on my face and flossed my teeth, clinging to my routine – to normal. I might have stayed in there, flossing forever, if I hadn't heard Liz say, "Oh. My. Gosh."

In the mirror I saw her staring at the picture on the screen with the eyes of a scientist, taking in every detail of the faces of the two boys.

"Cam," Liz called, without taking her eyes from the screen. "You've got to look at this!"

I moved from teeth-flossing to face-moisturising – anything to stay busy. "I've seen it already," I told her.

"No, Cam," Liz said, pointing at the bright screen in the dim room. "Look! Look at his shirt! Mr Solomon's T-shirt!"

But she didn't have to finish, because there... magnified – enhanced – I saw what I hadn't noticed in my

mom's office. I read the words BLACKTHORNE INSTITUTE
FOR BOYS.

"It's a school," Macey said slowly.

"*A boys' school!*" Liz cried.

I looked at the picture and said what everyone else
was thinking. "For spies?"

Chapter 6

I've always heard that the hardest thing for a spy isn't knowing things – it's acting like you *don't* know things you're not supposed to know. But I'd never really appreciated the difference until then. Looking at Mr Solomon was hard, talking to my mom was impossible, and the whole next day felt like a dream. A very weird there's-a-boys'-school-for-spies-that-nobody-ever-told-me-about nightmare.

Blackthorne was a school! That Mr Solomon had gone to! A school where they make more Mr Solomons! It was officially the strangest day of my entire covert life. (And that includes the time Dr Fibs's lab was temporarily gravity-free.)

I told myself that maybe it was just coincidence that Tina Walters had been swearing for years that there was a boys' school in Maine. After all, Tina also swore that Gillian Gallagher was a direct descendant of Joan of Arc. Tina swears a lot of things. Tina is frequently wrong.

But by the time Professor Buckingham took the podium and announced, "Today we will be reviewing the origins of the clandestine services, beginning with the Montevellian Theory of Operative Development," I knew I wasn't going to be waking up anytime soon.

I love Professor Buckingham. She's cool and strong and the most amazing role model, but her teaching style could probably best be described as…well…boring.

"Since its publication more than two thousand years ago, *The Art of War* has been the definitive thesis in warfare and deception…" she read from her notes as warm sunlight drifted through the windows and lunch grew heavy in my stomach. Her voice was soothing, like white noise, and my eyelids felt like they weighed about a ton, since, for obvious reasons, there hadn't been a whole lot of sleeping in our room the night before.

(Have I mentioned that we had evidence that strongly suggested there is a boys' school? For spies!)

But was Professor Buckingham filling us in about our long-lost band of potential brothers? No. She was talking about the 1947 Council of Covert Operatives, which, let me tell you, isn't nearly as interesting as it sounds.

Then Buckingham stopped talking. The sudden silence jolted me awake as my teacher looked over the top of her reading glasses. "Yes, Ms McHenry?"

And then, maybe for the first time that semester, Patricia Buckingham had our full attention.

"I'm sorry, Professor," Macey said. "I was only wondering – and I'm sorry if everyone else already knows this – I'm still a little new, you know."

"That is fine, Ms McHenry," Buckingham said. "What is your question?"

"Well, I was just wondering if there are other schools." Macey paused. She seemed to study our teacher a moment before adding, "Like the Gallagher Academy."

Liz almost fell out of her chair. Tina's eyes got really, really big, and I'm pretty sure the entire Tenth Grade class stopped breathing.

"I mean," Macey went on, "is this the only school of its kind, or are there—"

"There is only *one* Gallagher Academy for Exceptional Young Women, Ms McHenry," Buckingham said, throwing her shoulders back. "It is the finest institution of its kind in the world."

Buckingham smiled and returned to her notes, totally not expecting Macey to continue.

"So there *are* other institutions?"

Buckingham sighed, and an almost pained expression crossed her face as she carefully chose her words. "During the Cold War, the concept of recruiting and training operatives at a young age was not an uncommon practice.

And there *may* have been institutions formed for that purpose." Then she straightened her glasses and looked around the room as if to see exactly how far off course we'd forced her to stray. "For obvious reasons it is impossible to determine if any such schools are in existence now. If they ever existed at all, of course."

"So there *could* be other schools?" Tina exclaimed.

"*Could* and *are*, Ms Walters," Buckingham said, her voice as strong as steel, "are two very different things." She gave us a cold smile that signaled that the Q&A portion of the class was officially over.

Buckingham went back to her notes. "This theory was the fashion until 1953, when a group of retired agents…" Eva and Tina's attention drifted back out the window. But my roommates and I remained on high alert.

There have been other schools.

It doesn't mean there are any now.

I thought of the way Mr Solomon and my dad had been smiling in the picture. There was no date on it, no place. It was almost like it was a fake – part of some legend the CIA had manufactured in a lab, an alias of my father's that I had never known.

And then there was a knock at the door.

"Yes?" Buckingham said as she removed her glasses and the door eased open.

Every head in the room turned, and Mr Solomon said, "Pop quiz."

*

I hadn't exactly slept. I hadn't really eaten. It was maybe the worst possible time for a CoveOps assignment, and yet, three minutes later, as I buttoned my winter coat and ran down the Grand Staircase with the entire Tenth Grade CoveOps class, I stopped thinking about the picture and the file. I stopped thinking. And sometimes, even at the Gallagher Academy, that can be a very good thing.

The cold wind blew in our faces as we dashed through the front doors. A familiar van sat idling in the driveway, so we headed towards it until Mr Solomon called, "That's not our ride, ladies," and eight highly trained operatives skidded to a stop.

I looked to my right, expecting another van to appear from around the corner of the mansion, but all I saw were the eighth graders on their way to Protection & Enforcement class (P&E), their ponytails swaying back and forth as they ran. I turned to my left and saw nothing but snow in the vast open field that lay between the mansion and the woods.

"Then how are we…" I started, but then I trailed off. Bright sunlight bounced off slushy piles of half-melted snow. I squinted and blinked, making sure my eyes weren't playing tricks on me, because I could have sworn the ground's shape began to shift.

I glanced at my teacher, saw the faintest hint of a smile grow on his lips while, behind him, a great hollow opening

65

appeared in the middle of the field. Twin blades of a helicopter rose steadily from the huge hole, and wet snow whirled over the frozen ground as the blades started to spin. Mr Solomon pointed over his shoulder and said, "*That's* our ride."

Chapter 7

When I was five, Mom brought me to the Gallagher Academy for the first time. I'd thought it was the biggest building in the world; but today I looked through the helicopter's windows and watched the mansion grow smaller and smaller until it looked like it was in a snow globe that someone had given a good shake.

We flew so low over the woods that I could almost touch the trees. I thought about how my school had taught me chemistry and biology and even a very real appreciation for calligraphy. But helicopters were completely new territory! Was there going to be jumping? Or rappelling? (Hello – our uniforms have skirts.)

I don't know if it was turbulence, nerves, or the sight of the blindfolds in Mr Solomon's hands, but my stomach did a little flip.

"I'm afraid this isn't a sightseeing tour, ladies," Mr Solomon said as he placed the blindfolds over our eyes. "If I were you, I'd get comfortable. We're gonna be up here a while."

Well, it turns out "a while" is exactly forty-seven minutes and forty-two seconds, because that's how long it was until I felt the helicopter's quick descent. During that time, Mr Solomon had warned "No peeking, Ms Walters" twice, but other than that and Bex's snoring (she can sleep anywhere!), there wasn't a single sound on our mysterious ride.

I had no idea how fast we'd been going, or in what direction. All I knew was that we'd been in the air for almost forty-eight minutes and I really had to go to the bathroom.

We touched down. I heard the helicopter doors open, then someone guided me out onto concrete and into a waiting van. Soon we were off again. Destination unknown.

I smelled Bex's perfume beside me and drew some small comfort in the familiar scent.

"Blindfolds off," Mr Solomon said.

I tugged at the black band that circled my head, and soon I was squinting, trying to adjust to the light, the situation, and most of all, the sight of seven Gallagher Girls with very questionable hair. Static electricity filled the van. Eva's long black mane was practically standing on end. But

I was riveted by the state-of-the-art equipment that lined the windowless walls. Gadgets two generations better than anything we'd ever had were at our fingertips. I didn't need Joe Solomon to say, "Today we're playing with the pros, ladies" to know that it was true.

Mr Solomon turned to Courtney. "Countersurveillance has two functions, Ms Bauer, name them."

"Detect and evade surveillance procedures?" Courtney said, her answer sounding more like a question than a direct quote from page twenty-nine of *A Covert Operative's Guide to Surveillance Countermeasures.*

"That's right," Mr Solomon said. He didn't smile. He didn't say good job. Instead, he looked at the screens that filled the walls of the van, the wires and keyboards that were locked carefully into place. "It's a big world, ladies, but that doesn't make it easy to hide. If you stay on this course of study, you'd better be ready to look over your shoulders for the rest of your lives.

"Countersurveillance isn't something you learn from a book – it's not about theory," Solomon continued. "It's about the prickly feeling on the back of your neck, the little voice in your head that tells you when something isn't quite right." The van came to stop.

"Last semester, some of you" – he looked directly at me – "proved that you're pretty good at not being seen when you don't want to be. Well, today you go from being tail*ers* to tail*ees*. And, ladies..." Mr Solomon paused. My classmates were so still, so quiet, I could almost hear our pounding hearts. "This is harder."

I thought about our first mission last semester, how Mr Smith had used every countersurveillance measure known to man simply to enjoy a night in the Roseville town square. It had been exhausting just watching him, and I knew Mr Solomon was right. The bad guys could be anyone, they could be anywhere, and the odds would always be in their favour.

"Split up into four teams of two – and remember – I don't know exactly how many operatives are out there waiting today, ladies, but if they're good – and you should assume they're very, very good – then it will take every trick you know and every ounce of luck you can muster to identify them and lose them and make it to this location before five o'clock." He pulled an envelope from his coat pocket and placed it in Tina's hands.

He eased towards the back doors of the van. "Oh, and ladies, surveillance might help you do your job, but countersurveillance keeps you alive. If this Op is hard" – Mr Solomon's voice trailed off, and for a second he wasn't just a teacher, he was my father's friend – "it's supposed to be."

The doors swung open, bright sunlight streamed inside, and by the time we heard the heavy metal clank of the doors again, Joe Solomon was already gone.

We could have flown two hundred miles, or we could

have gone in circles and were now back in our school's driveway, twenty feet from where it had all began. Anything was possible, but one thing was sure: this quiz wasn't about marks – nothing at the Gallagher Academy ever really is.

"Do it, Cammie," Bex said. I eased towards the doors and opened one a crack.

A sliver of bright light sliced through the dim van as I peered outside and let my eyes adjust to what I saw. "It's the Mall."

"Cool," Bex said, sliding towards me.

I threw the door open wider. "Not that kind of mall."

Chapter 8

We crawled, one by one, out of the back of the van and stood for a long time, staring down the grassy promenade that ran between the the tall obelisk of the Washington Monument and the United States Capitol building where the American Congress meets, the heart of Washington, D.C. A lot of people think the Smithsonian is a museum, but it's actually a lot of different museums, and right then we were in the centre of them all. We could have gone to see artefacts from the U.S. Constitution document to the original Kermit the Frog puppets, but somehow I knew that, of all the school groups that take trips to the National Mall every year, ours was very different.

A man in black stretched his hamstrings on a bench before taking off in a jog. A long line of women wearing

matching sweatshirts that said "Louisville Ladies do D.C."
milled in front of a Metro stop. And I couldn't help
thinking, Oh, Mr Solomon is *good.*

After all, he'd been telling us for weeks that
surveillance is all about the home advantage, and that the
more limited a location's access is to the public, the easier
it will be to see someone who doesn't belong; but that
day, Joe Solomon had brought us to a place where
tourists converge from all over the world, a place that's
home to everyone from panhandlers to politicians (Macey,
by the way, swears there isn't much difference). And
before I knew it, Kim was saying exactly what I was
already thinking.

"We're being watched…"

"By friends of Mr Solomon's," Mick Morrison added
with a crack of her knuckles.

"And they could be…" Anna started, but her voice
broke and she swallowed hard.

"Anyone," Bex finished, her voice as excited as Anna's
was terrified.

Beside me, Tina was opening the envelope Mr
Solomon had given her.

"What?" Bex asked. "What does it say?"

Tina held up a folded brochure from the National
Museum of American History and pointed to a picture of
a tiny pair of bright red shoes. There was a message
scrawled across it:

There's No Place Like Home
5:00

Well, the girl in me has seen *The Wizard of Oz* approximately one billion times, so I knew that Dorothy's ruby slippers must be on the other side of the grassy lawn with the rest of our national treasures.

But the spy in me knew that getting there, tail-free, by five o'clock would be a whole lot harder than clicking our heels together and wishing for home.

"*And...*flip," Bex said an hour later.

We stopped midstride in front of the museum, then pivoted and started back in the opposite direction. The guy in the red baseball cap who had been following us since we passed the National Gallery of Art kept walking as if he didn't care that the two girls in front of him had just done a total about-face. And maybe he didn't. Care, I mean. But then again, maybe another member of his team had rotated into position and taken his place. There was no way of knowing. So we kept walking.

"We could be clear," Bex said, sounding wishful. "There might not be anyone on us."

"Or maybe there's a team of twenty CIA all-stars out here, and we're just not good enough to see them."

"Yeah," Bex said. "There's that, too."

I love being a pavement artist; seriously, I do. It's like

74

when guys who would normally hate being freakishly tall discover basketball, or when girls with abnormally long fingers sit down at a piano. Blending in, going unseen, being a shadow in the sun is what I'm good at. *Seeing* the shadows, it turns out, is not my natural gift.

"I can't believe I haven't seen anyone!" I said in frustration.

"Look at the bright side, Cam." Bex flung her arms out wide like a girl who'd cut class or run away from a school group. To the people around us, she no doubt looked beautiful and exotic – but not at all like a highly trained operative who was memorising the faces of every person who lingered within a hundred feet.

"We could be in Ancient Languages right now," she said, which was a very good point. "We could be locked in the basement with Dr Fibs." Which was an *excellent* point. (Since the X-ray goggles incident, our chemistry professor's lack of depth perception had made him even *more* accident-prone.) "And here the view is infinitely better."

I wish I could say she was talking about the Washington Monument or the Capitol or any of the sights that drive tourists to Washington. But I know Bex well enough to know she was really talking about a pair of boys who were sitting on a park bench thirty feet away, staring at her.

"Oooh," Bex said, throwing an arm around my shoulders. "*I want one.*"

"They're not puppies."

"Come on." She grabbed my hand. "Let's go talk to them. They're really cute!"

And…OK…I admit it: they *were* really cute. But this wasn't the time to encourage her. "Bex, we have a mission."

"Yeah, but we can multitask."

"No, Bex. Talking to civilian boys during a CoveOps exercise is a bad idea. Trust me." I forced a smile and added a singsong lilt to my voice as I said, "It's all fun and games until somebody gets their memory erased."

"Wow," Bex said. She blinked against the sun. "You're really…"

"What?" At that moment I knew there were at least nineteen security cameras trained on our path. I knew the Japanese man behind us was asking his wife if she still wanted a T-shirt from the Hard Rock Cafe. I knew a lot of things, but I didn't have a clue what my best friend was trying to say.

"I'm really what?" I asked again.

Bex glanced away, then back, and for one of the bravest people I know, she seemed almost afraid to say, "Not over Josh."

Josh. We'd been back at school for more than a week, but so far no one had said his name. And hearing it, to be honest, sounded strange.

"Of course I'm over him." I shrugged and started

walking, scanning the crowd. "*I* broke up with *him*. Remember? It wasn't a big deal."

Bex fell into step beside me. Her voice was almost timid as she said, "You don't have to pretend, Cam."

But that's what spies do – we pretend. We have aliases and disguises and go to great lengths to not be ourselves. So I said, "Of course I'm over him," and walked on, clinging to my cover till the end.

Bex probably would have argued with me; I'm sure she would have pointed out that Josh had been my first boyfriend, my first kiss; that he had seen me when to the rest of the world I was invisible, and that's not the kind of thing a girl – much less a spy – forgets so quickly. Knowing Bex, she probably would have pointed out a lot of things; but at that very moment…twenty feet ahead of us…we saw a woman in a beige business suit sitting on a bench, talking on a mobile phone. There was nothing unusual about her – not her hair, not her face. Nothing except for the fact that fifty minutes before, she'd been wearing a jogging suit and pushing a baby buggy.

"Bex," I said as calmly as possible.

"I see her," Bex replied.

Here's the thing you need to know about detecting and losing a tail: to do it right – I mean *really* right – you'd need to cover half a city. You'd climb in and out of taxis and train carriages and walk against the grain on at least a dozen busy pavements. You'd take all day.

But Mr Solomon hadn't given us all day, and that was kind of the point. So Bex and I spent the next hour going in one museum entrance and out another. Going up escalators only to come down the elevator two minutes later. We made sudden stops and looked in mirrors and tied our shoe-laces when they didn't need it. It was a virtual blur of corner-clearing and litter-dropping – everything I've ever seen, everything I've ever even heard of! (At one point Bex had almost talked me into crawling out the bathroom window in the Air and Space Museum, but a U.S. Marshal walked by and we decided not to push our luck.)

The seconds ticked by and the sun went lower, and soon the shadow of the Washington Monument was stretched almost the full length of the Mall. Time was running out.

"Tina," I said through my comms unit, "how are you and Anna?" But I was met with empty silence. "Mick," I said. "Are you there?"

Bex and I shared a worried glance, because there are reasons operatives go radio-silent, and most of them are not good.

We were cutting across the Mall, walking north, hoping anyone who wasn't intentionally following us would stick to the path.

"Forty-seven minutes," I announced, as if Bex weren't fully aware of that fact.

She turned around to glance at a man walking too fast behind us, and I didn't know whether to take it as an insult or a compliment that a team of CIA pros didn't care if they stood out anymore. They just wanted to stay with us.

When a crowd of girls filled the pavement in front of us and started down the long, steep escalator to the Metro station below, I looked at Bex. "Do it!" she said, and we merged into the crowd. The girls were wearing white blouses almost exactly like ours. Their name badges bore a logo from something called Mock Supreme Court. They were almost identical to us from the waist up, so Bex and I slipped off our coats as we descended into the cavernous, echoing station.

"I love your bracelet!" I said to the brunette next to me, because, while most girls are on to the whole strangers-with-candy thing, the strangers-with-compliments strategy is still remarkably effective.

"Thanks!" said the girl, who, according to her badge, was Whitney from Dallas. "Hey, are y'all with the group?"

"Yeah," Bex said. Then she looked down at her chest. "Oh my gosh! I left my name tag in my senator's office – we took them off to have our picture taken," she explained.

"Really?" another girl said. "That's cool. Who's your senator?"

And then Bex and I each said the first name that popped into our heads: "McHenry."

We looked at each other and shared a very subtle

laugh as the escalator carried us deeper and deeper beneath the city.

One of the girls, Kaitlin with a K, whispered to another girl, Caitlin with a C, "Are they back there?"

C peered back up the escalator, then grinned. "They are *so* following us!"

Bex and I might have exuded a panicked vibe about then, because K leaned in to explain, "These two hot guys have totally been checking us out."

"Oh," Bex said, as she and I used this as an excuse to check behind us. Sure enough, red-baseball-cap guy was back there (by now he was dressed like a navy lieutenant). And ten feet in front of him we saw the boys from the bench.

The C(K)aitlins started to laugh. It was hilarious. It was fun. Cute boys were on their tail, and maybe they thought they were being covert or cool, but all that really mattered was that once they got home they'd have a story they could tell. And it wouldn't be classified.

As the escalator entered the cavernous room, a train was already at the station. "Let's run and get it!" Bex screamed.

And everyone was off, racing to the bottom of the escalator, then dashing to the end of the train. The girls piled inside as the doors closed, and red-baseball-cap-slash-navy-officer guy jumped forward, barely making it into the next to last car as the train pulled out of the station, and away from where Bex and I stood underneath the escalator, waiting for our new friends and old shadow to disappear.

Bex and I watched the man in the train press himself against the glass as the train sped into the tunnel.

We were free.

We were clear.

We thought.

Chapter 9

Overconfidence is a spy's worst enemy, so to be on the safe side, Bex and I decided to split up when we left the Metro station. We had exactly twenty minutes to make it to the Museum of American History and our rendezvous with Mr Solomon. Twenty more minutes to make sure we really *were* clear.

I slipped into the shadows of the Metro station and watched Bex ascend the escalator, then waited long enough to be certain no one followed her. Then I headed to the elevator, but as I reached for the button, another hand beat me to it.

"Hey," one of the boys from the park bench said. He did that half head nod thing that all boys seem to do...or at least the boys I know. Which mainly means Josh.

"Hi," I replied, pushing the button again, hoping to

make the elevator come faster, because the last time a random boy had said hi to me, things had ended badly – like Mr-Solomon-practically-being-run-over-by-a-forklift badly. And needless to say, that's not the kind of thing that looks good on a girl's permanent record.

When the elevator doors slid open, I was kind of, sort of hoping he wouldn't step inside, but of course he did; and since the Metro station was forever and a day underground, the elevator ride was forever and a day long. The boy rested against the railing. He was slightly shorter and broader through the shoulders, but in the blurry reflection of the elevator doors, he almost looked like Josh.

"So," the boy said, pointing to the crest on my coat. "The Guggenheim Academy—"

"Gallagher Academy," I corrected.

"I've never heard of it."

Which was kind of the point, but I didn't say so. "Well, it's my school."

The elevator seemed to move slower and slower as the clock in my head ticked louder and louder, and I thought about how Mr Solomon might make us *walk* back to Roseville if no one achieved our mission objectives.

"You in a hurry or something?" the boy asked.

"Actually, I'm supposed to meet my teacher at the ruby slipper exhibit. I've only got twenty minutes, and if I'm late, he'll kill me." (Not a lie, but maybe an exaggeration – I hoped.)

"How do you know?"

"Because he said, 'Meet me at the ruby slipper exhibit.'"

"No." The boy was smiling, shaking his head. "How do you know you only have twenty minutes? You're not wearing a watch."

"My friend just told me." The lie was smooth and easy, and I was a little bit proud of it, happy that I didn't have to think about how, in forty-five seconds, this boy had noticed something Josh hadn't seen in four months.

"You fidget a lot," he said.

Make that two things Josh hadn't seen.

"I'm sorry," I said, but I wasn't. "I have low blood sugar." Lie number three. "I need to eat something." Which wasn't really a lie, since…well…I *was* hungry.

And then stranger-boy totally knocked me for a loop, because he handed me a bag of M&M's. "Here. I ate most of them already."

"Oh…um…" What was that I'd said about strangers with chocolate? "That's OK. Thanks, though."

He shoved the candy back in his pocket. "Oh," the boy said. "OK."

We finally reached the surface, and the doors slid open onto the Mall, where dusk had somehow fallen in the last ten minutes.

"Thanks again for the chocolate." I darted outside, knowing that to be safe I couldn't take the most direct way to the museum – not yet. I had to—

Wait.

I was being followed!

But not in any kind of covert sense!

"Where are you going?" I said, spinning on the boy behind me.

"I thought we were going to meet your teacher in the wonderful world of Oz."

"*We?*"

"Sure. I'm going with you."

"No you're not," I snapped, because A) The aforementioned *forklift thing,* and B) I'm pretty sure bringing a boy to a clandestine rendezvous isn't in the CIA handbook.

"Look," the boy said confidently. "It's dark. You're by yourself. And this *is* Washington D.C." Oh my gosh. It's like he had Grandma Morgan on speed-dial or something. "And you've only got" – he pondered it – "fifteen minutes to meet your teacher."

He was wrong by ninety seconds, but I didn't say so. All I knew was that I couldn't shake him – not without creating a lot more drama than letting him tag along was going to cause, so I just quickened my pace and said, "Fine."

As we walked against the cold wind, I told myself that this was good; this was fine. Nobody looking for a Gallagher Girl would expect me to be with a boy. He was cover. He was useful.

"You can really walk fast," he said, but I didn't say anything back. "So, do you have a name?" he asked, as if that were just the most innocent question ever. As if that isn't how broken hearts and broken covers always start.

"Sure. Lots of them."

That was probably the most truthful thing I'd told him yet, but the boy just smiled at me as if I were funny and flirty and cute. Let me tell you, I was none of those things, especially after not sleeping or eating, wearing a blindfold for an hour, then walking up and down the frozen Mall all day!

My nose was running. My feet were killing me. All I really wanted to do was get to Dorothy's slippers, click my heels together, and go home. But instead I had to put up with a boy who assumed I needed protecting. A boy with whom I could never "be myself". A boy who was staring at me as if he knew a secret – and worse – as if the secret was about me.

"Do you have a boyfriend?" he asked.

At this point I should point out that I was pretty sure the boy was flirting with me! Or at least I *thought* he was flirting with me, but without running it by Macey (and maybe plugging a sample into the voice-stress analyser that Liz had developed for this very purpose), there was no way I could be sure. Last semester I'd thought I was learning how to interpret boy-related things, but all I'd really learned was that Gallagher Girls shouldn't flirt with normal boys – not because we won't like them. But because we might like them too much. And that would be the worst thing of all.

"Look, thanks for the chivalry and all, but it really isn't necessary," I muttered what may have been the understatement of the century, since I'm pretty sure I could have killed him with my backpack. "It's just up here." I pointed to the Museum of American History, which stood gleaming twenty yards away. "And there's a cop over there."

"What?" the boy said, glancing at the D.C. police officer that stood at the corner of the street, "you think that guy can do a better job protecting you than I can?"

Actually, I thought *Liz* could have done a better job "protecting" me than he could, but instead I said, "No, I think if you don't leave me alone, I can scream and that cop will arrest you."

Somehow the boy seemed to know it was a joke… mostly. He stepped away and smiled. And for a moment I felt myself smile, too.

"Hey," I called to him, because, despite how annoying he was right then, a pang of guilt shot through my stomach. After all, he had been all knight-in-shining-armour*y*. It wasn't his fault I'm not the kind of girl who needs saving. "Thanks anyway."

He nodded. If it had been another day or I'd been another girl, a hundred other things might have happened. But I had begun the semester with a promise to be myself, and the real me was still a girl on a mission.

87

*

I darted for the doors and pushed my way inside, then slipped into a narrow hallway behind the help desk. I watched the entrance, waiting ninety seconds to be sure that I was clear.

"Bex." I tried my comms unit. "Courtney…Mick… Kim…" I told myself there was no way they'd *all* been made. They were probably downstairs in the ice-cream parlour; or maybe waiting in the van.

I grabbed a visitors' brochure from a stack on the help desk, slipped into a narrow stairwell, and began the three-storey climb to the slippers, not really caring that I wouldn't get to see the sights. (After all, the "Julia Child's Kitchen" exhibit didn't even illustrate how she used to send coded messages in her recipes.)

I could feel the ticking clock, almost see the look on Mr Solomon's face and hear him say well done. I was *so* close; I scanned the map and took the stairs two at a time until I emerged at the far end of the floor, where the ruby slippers were displayed.

There were no signs of Mr Solomon or my classmates; not another soul in the great oval room. I felt the clock in my head chime five o'clock. I stepped towards a case, which looked almost exactly like the one that stood in the centre of the Hall of History. But instead of the sword that Gillian Gallagher had used to kill the first guy who'd tried to assassinate President Lincoln, this case held a different kind of national treasure.

The ruby slippers were so small, so delicate, that a part of me wanted to marvel in the coolness of being that close to something so rare. The rest of me just wanted to know why seven Gallagher Girls had gone radio silent and my teacher was nowhere to be seen! Then I heard Mr Solomon's voice behind me.

"You're four seconds late."

The shoes glistened as I spun around. "But I'm alone."

"No, Ms Morgan. You're not."

And then the boy from the elevator, the boy from the bench, stepped out of the shadows.

And looked at me.

And smiled.

And said, "Hi again, Gallagher Girl."

Chapter 10

There are changes that come slowly – like evolution. And letting your hair grow out. And then there are changes that happen in a second – with a ringing phone, a well-timed glance. And in that moment I knew the Gallagher Academy wasn't alone. I knew there was a school for boys. And, most of all, I knew one of them had just got the best of me.

This can't be happening, I chanted in my head. This can't be—

"Nice work, Zach," Mr Solomon said. "Zach" winked at me, and I thought, This is totally happening!

I'd been sloppy. I'd been distracted. And worst of all, I'd let a boy stand between me and my mission objectives…again.

The whole thing might have been too awful – too

humiliating – to endure if I hadn't summoned the courage to say, "Hi, Blackthorne Boy." Since I wasn't supposed to know the Blackthorne Institute for Boys even existed, there was a split second when I had the upper hand.

Mr Solomon blinked. Zach's mouth gaped open, and I was the person smiling when my teacher said, "Very good, Ms Morgan." But then he looked at the boy who had beaten me at my own game, and my face went as red as Dorothy's shoes. "But not good enough."

I saw the day like a movie in my mind: Zach and his friend watching Bex twirl in the breeze; the boys standing on the long escalator ride into the Metro station. They'd been there – we'd seen them! But we'd thought they were just…boys. And they were. Kind of like we're just girls.

"Your mission was…what?" I started, amazed by how even my voice sounded, how steady my pulse felt. "To keep us from achieving our mission?"

The boy cocked his head and raised his eyebrows. "Something like that." Then he smirked and exhaled a half laugh. "I thought I could just make you late for your meeting. I didn't think you'd actually tell me where it was and walk me halfway there."

I thought I was going to be sick – seriously – right there in front of eight security cameras, my favourite teacher, and…Zach.

I'd thought he was chivalrous (but he wasn't). I'd thought he was cute (but tall, dark, and handsome is highly overrated when you think about it). And worst of all, I'd thought he'd been flirting…with me.

A group of tourists wandered into the shoe exhibit and pressed closer to the case. I was jostled by the crowd, then blinded by a flashing camera. Mr Solomon put his arm around my shoulders and guided me to the doors.

I looked back towards the slippers.

But Zach was already gone.

How weird was the helicopter ride home? Let me count the ways:

In an effort to make themselves less tailable, Mick and Eva had traded their school uniforms for jumpsuits from the National Park Service maintenance staff.

Kim Lee had fallen down the stairs at the National Gallery, so she had to sit with her ice-packed ankle propped on Tina's lap.

Courtney Bauer was still wet, following a very unfortunate Lincoln Memorial Reflecting Pool incident.

And Anna Fetterman kept staring into the dark with her mouth open because, of all the Gallagher Girls on the Mall that day, she was the only one to achieve our mission objective (yeah, you read that right, *Anna Fetterman!*), and she was the most shocked person of all.

Even Bex had picked up a tail on her way out of the Metro station and didn't make it to the museum on time.

So that's why the entire sophomore CoveOps class

from the Gallagher Academy for Exceptional Young Women sat in silence, watching the Washington Monument fade into the dark night while the helicopter rose, carrying us home.

I thought there would be questions. And theories. But even Tina Walters – the girl who had once hacked into a National Security Agency satellite in order to look for the alleged boys' school – didn't have a thing to say.

After all, it's one thing to learn there's a top-secret school for boy spies.

It's another to find out they might be better than you.

The countryside shimmered beneath us, and the mansion finally came into view, lights shining through the windows and reflecting off the snow.

I felt the helicopter touch down, saw the snow swirl around us as Mr Solomon reached for the helicopter door, then paused.

"Today I asked you to do something that maybe fifty people in the entire world can do," he said, and I thought, This is it – a pep talk, a debrief. Or at least an explanation of who those boys were and why we were meeting them now. But instead, Mr Solomon said, "By the end of this semester, there had better be fifty-eight."

"You really saw some?" Liz said an hour later. Sure, we had the stereo blaring and the shower running, but Liz still whispered, "They really…exist?"

"Liz," I whispered back. "They're not unicorns."

"No," Bex said flatly, "they're boys. And they're…good."

Dampness weighed my hair, steam fogged the bathroom mirror, but the four of us kept the door closed, because A) Steam is excellent for your pores. And B) The biggest news in the history of our sisterhood was sweeping through the halls of a place where eavesdropping is both an art and a science. So needless to say, my roommates and I weren't taking any chances.

"Maybe it's not what you think," Liz said. "Maybe they weren't from Blackthorne at all. Maybe they just looked young. Maybe—"

"Oh," Bex said simply, "it was them."

As I dropped to the edge of the bathtub and rested my head in my hands, I knew nothing hurt as much my pride.

"I can't believe I actually talked to him," I finally admitted. "I can't believe I actually *told* him where I was going!"

"It couldn't have been that bad, Cam," Liz said, dropping to sit beside me.

"Oh, it was worse! He was…and I was…and then…" But I gave up because, in all of my fourteen languages, there wasn't a single word that could express the anger-slash-humiliation that was coursing through my veins.

"So," Macey said, hopping onto the counter and crossing her long legs, "just how hot was this guy?"

Oh. My. Gosh.

"Macey!" I moaned. "Does it matter?"

Bex nodded. "He was pretty hot."

"Guys," I pleaded, "the hotness is really beside the point."

"But exactly what kind of hot was he?" Liz asked as she pulled open her notebook and grabbed a pen. "I mean, would you say he was pretty-boy hot, like Leonardo DiCaprio the early years, or ruggedly-handsome hot, like George Clooney the later years?"

I was about to remind her that neither kind of hot could justify my revealing the location of a clandestine rendezvous, when Bex answered for me. "Rugged. Definitely rugged." Macey nodded her approval.

Down the hall, the rest of the sophomore class was hacking into the Smithsonian surveillance system and running the pictures of every male between the ages of twelve and twenty-two who had been on the Mall that day through the FBI's facial recognition program. At least a dozen girls were in the library scouring the very books we had abandoned days before.

Still, no one had said the name Blackthorne. No one had mentioned the East Wing.

Liz closed her notebook. "Well, now we know what your mom and Mr Solomon were talking about. And it's over." She smiled. "You never have to see him again."

Then she seemed to consider the naiveté of what she'd just said. "Do you?"

*

By 4 am I was seriously starting to resent Joe Solomon and
all of his "use your memory" training, because at that point
I would have given my entire life savings (which were
$947.52) to forget what had happened.

Bex was lying in the light of the window, smiling
a devilish smile, probably dreaming of hostile takedowns
and elaborate covers. Liz was curled up against the wall,
taking up no more room than a doll, and Macey lay on her
back sleeping peacefully despite the wheezing sound of air
rushing past the great big diamond in her nose. But me?
All I could do was stare at the ceiling and pray for sleep,
until I finally threw off my covers and brought my bare feet
to the cold hardwood floor.

I swear I didn't know where I was going. Seriously.
I didn't. I just slipped on a pair of trainers – no socks – and
crept towards the door.

Every spy knows that sometimes you just have to go
on adrenaline and instinct, so when I found myself
wandering the dark empty hallways, I didn't ask why.
When I started down the second-floor corridor, I didn't tell
myself to turn around.

Moonlight fell through the stained glass windows at
the far end of the corridor. I crept towards the tall
bookcase at the mouth of the Hall of History and the
hidden passageway it conceals. Then I heard the floor
creak behind me and saw the beam of a flashlight burn

through the hall before shining in my face. I threw my hands over my eyes and started preparing alibis. (I was sleepwalking…I needed a glass of water….I'd dreamed that I hadn't turned in my COW homework for Mr Smith and was going to check…)

"You didn't think we'd let you go without us, did you?" Bex asked.

When Macey finally lowered the flashlight, I could see Liz shivering in her thin nighty and Bex holding open a small black case; her trusty silver lock picks shimmered in the light.

No one had to say where we were going. We'd started down the path days before and were finally going to see where it ended. While Bex worked on the lock to the East Wing, I didn't look into the Hall of History; I didn't look at my mom's dark office; and most of all, I didn't think about all the promises I was no longer in the mood to keep.

"Got it," Bex said in record time, and then the door swung open.

We stepped into a hallway we used to know. Now it led to a large open room. Deserted classrooms ringed the space, but the desks were gone. A door stood open, and I could see that a bathroom had been modified to stand between two…bedrooms? The scent of sawdust and fresh paint filled the air.

"They look like…" Liz started but trailed off.

"Bedrooms?" she said, her genius mind trying to wrap itself around such a simple fact.

There were beds and desks and wardrobes. The rogue-florists theory didn't seem scary anymore. "You know what this means?" Bex asked.

There was only one thing it could mean.

"Boys," I said. "Boys are coming to the Gallagher Academy."

"Yeah." Bex smiled. "And we're going to get a rematch."

Chapter 11

The Gallagher Academy is a school for exceptional young *women* for a reason. Actually, lots of reasons.

For example, by having only girls' bathrooms (not counting the faculty lounges), the mansion is able to devote valuable square footage to things like chemistry labs and TV rooms.

Also, the average teenage girl in a mixed educational environment is likely to spend one hundred hours a year getting ready for school, when that time *could* be used for sleeping or studying or debating the merits of foot vs. vehicular surveillance in an urban setting.

But the biggest reason the Gallagher Academy is a school for girls is that in the late 1800s it was perfectly acceptable for boys to learn maths and science and how to hold their own in a duel, while girls like Gillian Gallagher were forced to master the fine art of needlepoint.

Gilly couldn't join the Secret Service – even after she'd saved the life of a president – because the other agents were afraid her hoopskirt might get in the way (when, in truth, hoopskirts were excellent for smuggling sensitive information and/or weapons).

So Gilly did the next best thing: she opened a school where proper young ladies could learn all the things they were never supposed to need, a place where young women were free to become exceptional without the pressure or influence of boys.

But now...more than a century later...all of that was going to change.

At breakfast the next morning, my roommates and I stared at our plates, not really listening as Anna Fetterman recounted the day before in detail.

"Und dann sah ich ihn in den Wandschrank gehn and ich wusste, dass ich ihn dort einschliessen musste um dann die Stufen hin unter gehen zu koennen." she said, and I have to admit, locking the agent on her tail inside a cupboard at the top of the Washington Monument was pretty ingenious of her, but I was in no mood to take notes.

"Cammie. When do you think they'll...you know..." Liz whispered, despite the sign telling us we were supposed to be speaking in German. "Come?"

I didn't have a clue. In the last twenty-four hours, the entire world as I knew it had changed, so I wasn't in a hurry to give the boys' arrival a time frame – to make it in any way real.

But then the reality of the situation stopped being an optional thing.

My mom rose from the staff dining table and took the podium. "Excuse me, ladies, but I have an announcement to make."

The doors at the back of the room swung open.

I knew that nothing at the Gallagher Academy for Exceptional Young Women would ever be the same again.

Forks dropped. Heads turned. For the first time in twelve hours, there wasn't a single whisper inside our stone walls.

Gallagher Girls are supposed to be prepared for anything and everything. Even though I'm pretty sure we could handle an invasion by enemy forces, one glance at my classmates told me that not a single Gallagher Girl felt fully prepared for the sight of fifteen boys standing in the doorway of the Grand Hall.

Boys were looking at us. Boys were walking towards us. It's one thing to *know* that boys are coming...someday. It's quite another to be enjoying a nice, relaxing meal and then turn around to see a mob of teenage testosterone moving your way! (I mean, hello, I was wearing the skirt with the stain on the butt.)

But did my mom seem to care about that? No. She just gripped the podium at the front of the room and said, "The

Gallagher Academy for Exceptional Young Women has a proud history…" I'm pretty sure no one was listening.

"For more than a hundred years, this institution has remained secluded, but yesterday, some of your classmates were able to meet another set of exceptional students from another exceptional institution." I guess *meet* is code for *be humiliated by*.

"Members of the Gallagher trustees, along with the board of directors from the Blackthorne Institute, have long thought that our students would have a lot to learn from each other." She smiled. A strand of dark hair fell across her face, and she tucked it behind her ear before looking across the massive room. "And this year we're going to see it happen."

Tina Walters looked like she was going to pass out; Eva Alvarez was holding her orange juice halfway between the table and her mouth – but Macey McHenry seemed to have barely noticed that boys were walking past the Tenth Grade table. She glanced up from her organic chemistry flash cards for about a millisecond and said, "That's them?" She shrugged. "I've seen cuter." And then she went back to her notes.

"When Gillian Gallagher was a girl, this hall had been home to balls and dances, friends and family, but it hasn't had many guests in the last century," Mom said. "I'm so glad today is an exception."

Then for the first time, I realised that the boys were

not alone. There was a man ushering them to the front of the room. He had a round, reddish face and a bright, wide smile, and as he walked down the centre aisle, he actually waved and shook hands with the girls he passed, as if he were a game show contestant and my mom had just asked him to "Come on down".

"It's my pleasure to introduce Dr Steven Sanders. Dr Sanders…" Mom started, but trailed off as the little man walked behind the staff table, tilted the microphone towards his mouth, and said, "Dr Steve."

"Excuse me?" Mom asked.

"Call me *Dr Steve*," he said with a punch at the air.

I looked at Liz, suspecting that the thought of calling a teacher by his first name would send her into shock, but she didn't seem to notice anything beyond the boys who stood near the head table.

"Of course," Mom told him, then turned to face us. "*Dr Steve* and his students will be spending the remainder of the semester with us."

At this, a low chorus of whispers grew inside the hall. "They will be attending your classes, eating with you at meals." Sleeping in the East Wing, I thought.

"Ladies, this is a wonderful opportunity," Mom finished. "And I hope you will use this time to forge bonds of friendship that you can carry throughout your lives."

"I wouldn't mind being bonded to him," Eva Alvarez

said, gesturing to a boy at the edge of the pack. A boy with dark brown hair and broad shoulders.

A boy who crossed his arms and leaned against the head table.

A boy who was smiling.

At me.

Chapter 12

"Members of this tribe can be identified by what physical characteristic, Ms Bauer?" Mr Smith asked an hour later, but I'm pretty sure I speak for the entire Tenth Grade class when I say that we were far less interested in the countries of the world than we were in what was going on in our own school. I mean, how were we supposed to focus when there were extra chairs at the back of our classroom? Chairs that were waiting...for boys.

Even Liz kept looking around as if the boys were going to teleport into the back of the room or something. But Mr Smith kept lecturing like this was an ordinary day – right up until a deep voice called "Knock knock," and Dr Steve pushed open the door.

Dr Steve exclaimed, "Good morning, ladies," except that, if you ask me, it wasn't. And I was just getting ready to say so, when the morning got worse. Way worse. Because, not only had Dr Steve barged in, interrupting a perfectly nice lecture, but he hadn't come alone.

Three boys stood behind him: one was skinny with glasses and thick black hair. One bore a striking resemblance to your average Greek god. And standing between them...was Zach.

My friends call me the Chameleon – I'm the girl who blends in, who goes unseen – but I have never wanted to be invisible as much as I did then.

I mean, I get the interschool co-operation thing; I can totally grasp the concept of camaraderie and teamwork. But the spy in me had been beaten the day before, and the girl in me had been flirted with and used. I slumped in my chair, wishing Bex were still using that volumising conditioner, because at the moment, I needed all the cover I could get.

"Can I help you, Dr Sanders?" Mr Smith asked, not even trying to hide the impatience in his voice, but Dr Steve just looked at him and held one hand in the air as if he were trying to put his finger on something.

"I say, your voice sounds so familiar." Dr Steve said. Mr Smith is one of the most wanted (not to mention paranoid) ex-spies in the world, and every summer he goes to the CIA's official plastic surgeon and gets a whole new face, so there was no way Dr Steve was going to recognise him. "Have we met before?"

"No," Mr Smith said coolly. "I'm quite sure we haven't."

"Never did any work at the Andover Institute, did you?"

"No," Mr Smith said again, then started back towards the board as if his lecture had been delayed long enough.

"Oh well," Dr Steve said with a laugh. Then he pointed to the boys behind him. "Shall we have the boys introduce themselves?"

"I have learned, Dr Sanders—"

"Steve," Dr Steve corrected, but Mr Smith carried on, not even pausing for breath.

"—that ours is an occupation where names are – at best – temporary," Mr Smith finished. Which, when you think about it, is putting it mildly coming from a man who (according to Tina Walters) has one hundred and thirty-seven aliases registered with the CIA. "But, if they must…" Mr Smith rolled his eyes and sat on the corner of his desk.

The skinny boy stepped forward, pulling nervously on his tie as if it were an entirely new kind of torture.

"Um…I'm Jonas," he said, shifting from foot to foot. "I'm sixteen. I'm a sophomore—"

"Thus your enrolment in this class," Mr Smith said drily. "Welcome, Jonas. Please have a seat."

"Excellent job, Jonas." Dr Steve said, ignoring Mr Smith, who had started to hand out a pop quiz. "Excellent job. Now, Jonas here is on the research track of study. I don't suppose any of you young ladies could show Jonas around?"

"Humph!" Liz exclaimed, which probably had less to do with the fact that she was eager to show Jonas around than the fact that Bex had just kicked the back of her chair (hard). But Dr Steve didn't see any of that. He pointed at Liz and said, "Excellent!" again.

(Note to self: "excellence" at the Blackthorne Institute is probably marked on a very different scale than the one we use at the Gallagher Academy.)

"Jonas, you can spend the day with Ms…" Dr Steve looked to Liz.

"Sutton. Liz Sutton."

"Excellent," Dr Steve said one more time. "Now, Grant, if you would—"

"I'm Grant," said the boy on Zach's other side. Grant didn't look like a sophomore – Grant looked like Brad Pitt's body double.

He slid into the seat beside Bex, who smiled and tossed her hair in a move that they don't teach in P&E.

Oh my gosh! Is this what it's like to have class with boys? I mean, I know I *used* to go to school with boys before I started at the Gallagher Academy, but there really isn't that much hair-tossing in kindergarten. (Although, I do remember some hair-pulling that resulted in some *real* tossing, but then Mom forbade me from using the Wendelsky Manoeuvre on civilians ever again.)

One boy remained at the front of the room, but instead of waiting for Dr Steve, Zach walked to the back of the class. "I'm Zach," he said, sliding into the chair behind Grant – the one next to me – "and I think I've found my guide."

From the front of the room I faintly heard the word. "Excellent!" but I didn't necessarily agree.

Gallagher Girls have missions – hard ones. All the time. But as soon as COW was over, I gathered my books and fought the feeling that I was completely unprepared for what I had to do. As I started for the door I told myself all the reasons I shouldn't feel the way I was currently feeling:

1. In the clandestine services it does help to have as many allies as possible, so knowing a Blackthorne Boy or two could come in handy someday.
2. Mr Solomon had been a Blackthorne Boy (and maybe my dad had been too). They turned out all right.
3. As Liz had previously stated, having unlimited access to boys could be a good thing, scientifically speaking.
4. Zach had only been following orders on the Mall the day before.
5. He'd been nice.
6. He'd offered me chocolate.
7. It wasn't his fault he'd been…better than me.

*

"So, we meet again."

Yes, Zach actually said that, even though, if you wanted to be technical about it, we hadn't actually *met* in Washington. Not really. I mean, *his* cover identity had spoken to *my* cover identity, but talking to someone who doesn't know you're a spy is completely different from standing together in the middle of your top-secret school of covert learning.

Girls pressed against us from all directions, like a tide that was going out and coming in at the same time, but Zach and I didn't get caught up in the current.

He surveyed the great stone walls and ancient pillars that surrounded him. "So *this* is the famous Gallagher Academy."

"Yes," I replied politely. I *was* his guide, after all, not to mention someone who's had three and a half years of Culture and Assimilation training. "This is the second-floor corridor. Most of our classes are down this hall."

But Zach wasn't listening. Instead, he was staring – at me. "And *you're*..." he started slowly, "...the famous Cammie Morgan."

OK, first of all, I have no idea how Zach knew my name, but that wasn't as intriguing as the way he seemed oblivious to the crashing bodies and whispering girls.

Josh used to look at me like he wanted to kiss me, or laugh at me, or get psychiatrists to study me – all of which

I totally preferred to the look Zach was giving me then, not as if I were famous, but as if I were *infamous*. And when you're the girl who's known for being invisible, there's nothing quite as scary as being seen.

"Come on," I mumbled, after what seemed like a very long time. I started down the hall. "Culture and Assimilation is on the fourth floor."

"Whoa," he said, stopping suddenly. "Did you just say you're taking me to *culture* class?" he asked, a mocking smile growing on his lips.

"Yes."

And then Zach grinned. "Boy, when they say you've got the toughest curriculum in the world...they *mean* it." But it didn't take a genius to know *he* didn't mean it. At all.

I told myself he was there to "forge friendships". I reminded myself that I'd promised my mom I wouldn't break any more rules (and I'm pretty sure pushing visiting students down the stairs is frowned upon). I called on every ounce of strength and composure I possessed as I started towards the fourth floor, pushing through the crowds. "Culture and Assimilation has been a part of the Gallagher curriculum for more than a hundred years, Zach."

We turned down the corridor to the tea room. "A Gallagher Girl can blend into any culture – any environment. Assimilation isn't a matter of social graces." I stopped in the hallway with my hand against the door frame. "It's a matter of life and death."

I thought I'd made a pretty good point, and the condescending look had just started to fade from Zach's face when gentle strains of music came floating into the hall. I heard Madame Dabney say, "Today, ladies and gentlemen, we will be studying the art of...the dance!"

And then Zach leaned down; I felt his breath warm against my ear as he whispered, "Yeah... Life. And. Death."

I stepped into the tea room and saw that the silk curtains had been pushed away from the tall windows that lined the room's far side, and a bouquet of fresh orchids sat atop the grand piano. Chairs and linen-covered tables circled the edge of the room, and Madame Dabney stood alone beneath the crystal chandelier. Our teacher floated across the gleaming parquet floor, a monogrammed handkerchief in her hands, as she said, "I have been saving this very special class for the arrival of our very special guests."

"Did you hear that?" Zach whispered. "I'm special."

"That's a matter of—" I started, but before I could finish, Madame Dabney said, "Oh, Cameron dear, would you and your friend like to demonstrate for the rest of the class?"

What I wanted to do was disappear, but Madame Dabney pulled us into the centre of the tea room. "You must be Zachary Goode. Welcome to the Gallagher Academy. Now, I must ask that you place your right hand firmly in the centre of Cameron's lower back." Even a highly trained pavement artist can't hide when the person they're hiding from has his arm around her waist.

"OK, now. Everyone find a partner," Madame Dabney instructed. "Yes, girls, some of you will have to take turns being the boy."

I heard my friends scurrying around me. There was laughing and giggling, and I saw Jonas and Liz manage to step on each other's feet at the exact same time, while Zach and I stood in the centre of the room, waiting for further instructions.

"Ladies," Madame Dabney said, "you will place your right hand firmly in your partner's palm." I did it.

"What's the matter, Gallagher Girl?" Zach said, eyeing me. "You're not actually mad about yesterday, are you?"

The music grew louder; I heard my teacher say, "Now, ladies and gentlemen, we will begin with a basic box step. No, Rebecca, if you're going to dance with Grant, then you *must let him lead*!"

But Zach was smiling at me, and a knowing look filled his eyes. "It was a cover, Gallagher Girl. An op. Maybe you're familiar with the concept?"

But before I could say anything, Madame Dabney placed one hand on Zach and the other on me and announced, "Hold your partners tightly." She pushed us closer together, and before I knew it, we were dancing.

Chapter 13

Life at spy school has never been boring (for obvious reasons), but the next two weeks were some of the busiest of my entire future-government-operative existence. It was practically all I could do to A) Avoid Zach. B) Keep up with my classwork. And C) Keep all the rumours separate from the facts. For example:

The Blackthorne delegation consisted of fifteen boys ranging in age from Eighth Grade to senior. FACT.

One of the boys was the son of an infamous double agent, and the CIA had faked his death and legally adopted him in order to develop him as a sleeper operative. RUMOUR.

Dr Steve had broken Madame Dabney's heart in a bitter love triangle with a Pakistani belly dancer in the Champagne region of France. RUMOUR (probably).

And two things were absolutely, positively true: 1) There was so much talking in the common room at all hours of the night that even a highly dedicated operative couldn't get much sleep. And 2) Early morning grooming rituals start way earlier at a school where actual boys attend.

So that's why I was struggling to keep my eyes open as I sat down beside Macey in the Grand Hall one Friday morning.

"Did you know that Jonas was a finalist for the Fieldstein Honour last year?" Liz asked in Japanese but then switched to English. "Isn't that really...wow."

At the end of the table, Courtney Bauer and Anna Fetterman were making plans to highlight each other's hair using materials from the chemistry labs. (Note to self: never let Courtney Bauer and Anna Fetterman near your hair.) Mick Morrison and Bex were talking about a truly impressive Mankato Manoeuvre that Grant had demonstrated the day before in P&E.

Then someone pushed onto the bench beside me. "*Ne*, Cammie, *Zach toha donattenno*?" Tina Walters asked.

OK, at this point I should probably point out that it was early, I hadn't got a lot of sleep the night before, and different phrases can take on very different meanings in foreign languages; but despite all that, I could have sworn that Tina Walters had just asked me if there was "something going on" with me and Zach. And I'm pretty sure that by "something", she wasn't referring to any kind of extra credit assignments!

"Tina!" I gasped, because I could see that Zach was only twenty feet away, deep in conversation with Mr Solomon at the waffle bar. "What are you talking about?"

"You know," Tina said, nudging me. "Don't look now. He's staring at you."

Well, I don't know how normal girls react to the "Don't look now" command, but spy girls are trained to find the nearest reflective surface (which was the sterling-silver orange juice jug) *and look*.

Zach *was* studying me. But Mr Solomon was, too.

"So," Tina asked again, "do you like him?"

She couldn't be serious. Then I looked up and down the long table of eavesdropping girls, and realised *she was totally serious*!

I couldn't believe she was asking me that. In the Grand Hall. With boys...*everywhere*! It was as if Tina didn't know that it's standard protocol to do a basic security sweep and activate a bug scrambler before engaging in conversations that classified. I mean, sure, it *was* pretty loud in here, but the Blackthorne Institute could very well have an excellent lip-reading curriculum.

But did Tina consider that? No. She just leaned closer, looking almost as excited as the time she'd found out Professor Buckingham had spent the summer organising security for Prince William, and said, "Because, according to my research, you technically have dibs on Zach, since you talked to him first. If you want him."

Gallagher Girls study. We prepare. We never do anything halfway. But most of all, we don't let anyone – not even fifteen Blackthorne Boys – come between us.

"Tina," I said slowly as I leaned over the table and practically whispered the words, "I officially relinquish my claim to Zach."

Tina smiled and nodded. Everyone went back to breakfast.

"They'll get over it."

The voice was so faint I thought I might have dreamed it. Then I saw Macey McHenry – the girl who had actually been stopped on the streets of New York and offered a shot at being on the cover of *Vogue* – sitting there in a wrinkled uniform with her hair in a ponytail, reading the newest *Journal of Extreme Extractions.*

"The boy thing – the new – it'll wear off," Macey said, not noticing that three boys at the Eighth Grade table were staring at her, not caring that she was the only girl in the entire room without a trace of makeup.

It was as if a virus had been injected into our school, but Macey'd known about a thousand boys before she'd come here. And I'd known Josh. The two of us had been exposed to boys before, so we had built up antibodies. We were, in a word, immune.

*

I'm not completely sure, and this isn't scientific or anything, but I think the most exciting words in the English language might be *CoveOps class, let's go.* Or at least that's what I thought as the elevator opened into Sublevel One that day, and I saw Mr Solomon walking towards us, pulling on a jacket.

He didn't tell us to open our textbooks; he didn't have us take our seats; instead, he led us upstairs and through the open doors, into the crisp cool air towards one of the ruby-red shuttle vans with the Gallagher crest on its side. I know this might sound a little anticlimactic after the helicopter thing, but to be honest, being in a helicopter with seven of my sisters was relaxing compared to the feeling of sitting in the back of the van…with boys.

Grant sat beside Mr Solomon at the front of the van. Zach was on the other side of Mr Solomon, his breathing steady and even, and I knew that the Blackthorne Institute had either trained him very well or very poorly, because he seemed indifferent to the fact that he was locked in the back of a van with eight expertly trained teenage girls, a man who (according to Tina) had once strangled a Yugoslavian arms dealer with a pair of control-top tights, and…Dr Steve.

"I say, Mr Solomon," Dr Steve droned on, "you've done an excellent job with these young ladies. Just excellent."

Mr Solomon had lectured on rolling exits the week

before, and for a second I wondered if he'd brought us here to illustrate how to throw someone out of a moving van; but then I remembered that Dr Steve was driving.

"You ladies need to pay attention to this man," Dr Steve said. "He's a living legend."

"Just as long as they remember the most important part of that is the *living*," Mr Solomon said.

I felt the van stop at our front gates then turn right and start down a road I knew well.

"Today's about the basics, ladies and gentlemen," Mr Solomon said easily, as if the *gentlemen* had always been there. "I want to watch you move; see you work together. Pay attention to your surroundings, and remember – half of your success in this business comes from looking like you belong, so today your cover is that you're a bunch of private-school students enjoying a trip to town."

I thought about the Gallagher Academy logo on the side of this particular van, then glanced down at my uniform – made a mental note of what version of myself I was supposed to be, while, beside me, Bex asked, "What are we really?"

"A bunch of spies" – Mr Solomon pulled a coin from his pocket and gave it a flip – "playing tag." Before the coin had even landed in his palm, I knew it wasn't a matter of heads or tails.

"Brush pass, Ms Baxter," Mr Solomon said. "Define it."

"The act of covertly passing an object between two agents."

"Correct," Mr Solomon said. I glanced at Zach, half expecting him to roll his eyes or something, because, frankly, brush passes aren't that much more complicated than learning to waltz with Madame Dabney. If you want to be technical about it, brush passes are about as low tech as you get; but they're important, or else Mr Solomon wouldn't have loaded us into the van that day. "The little things can get away from you, ladies and gentlemen. The little things matter."

"So right you are," Dr Steve chimed from the front seat. "As I was telling Headmistress Morgan just this—"

"It's you and the street today," Mr Solomon said, ignoring Dr Steve. "Today's test might be low tech, but this is trade craft at its most essential."

He pulled a small box from beneath his seat, and I instantly recognised the cache of comms units and tiny cameras that were concealed within pins and earrings, tie clips and silver crosses exactly like the one I'd worn last semester.

"Watch. Listen," Mr Solomon said. "Remember to communicate. Observe."

Kim Lee was struggling to pin an American flag–pin-slash-camera onto her coat, and then Grant said, "Allow me," and Kim batted her eyelashes and swooned a little (yes – actual swoonage) as he helped her.

"Pair off," Solomon continued his instructions as the van stopped. "Blend in, and remember, we'll be watching."

I looked at Bex and started for the doors, but before I could put a foot outside, Mr Solomon said, "Oh no, Ms Morgan. I believe you already have a partner."

It shouldn't have been that hard – not the brush passes, not the questions Mr Solomon fired through our comms units at regular intervals. None of it. But as I climbed out of the van I knew this was going to be one of the toughest assignments I'd ever been on. Because, for starters, at 11 am on a Friday morning, there isn't a lot of pedestrian traffic on the town square in Roseville, Virginia, and everyone knows pedestrian traffic is key when trying to covertly pass something between two agents.

Also, despite the bright sun and cloudless sky, it was still pretty cold outside, so I could either wear gloves and potentially inhibit my coin-handling ability, or go gloveless and allow my hands to freeze.

And, of course, there is the fact that your partner is your lifeline during covert operations, and at that moment, my partner was Zach.

"Come on, Gallagher Girl," he said as he headed for the square. "This should be fun."

But it didn't sound like fun – at all. Fun is movie marathons; fun is experimenting with fourteen kinds of ice cream and creating your own custom flavour. Fun is *not* hanging out in the place where I had met, kissed, and broken up with the world's sweetest boy. And participating in a clandestine training exercise with a different boy who wasn't sweet at all.

The gazebo still stood in the centre of the square. The cinema was behind me, and the Abrams and Son Pharmacy – Josh's family's business – was exactly where it had been for seventy years. Things are supposed to look different when you come back, but despite the sight of my classmates walking two by two along pavements, everything was exactly as I'd remembered. Not even the handbags displayed in the Anderson's Accessories window had changed; for a second it felt like the past two months hadn't happened.

"So," Zach said as he stretched out on the steps of the gazebo, "come here often?"

The loose stone where Josh and I had hidden our notes – my first dead-letter drop – was just a foot away so I shrugged and said, "I used to, but then the deputy director of the CIA made me promise to stop." Zach laughed a quiet, half-laugh as he squinted up at me through the sun.

In my earpiece, I heard Mr Solomon say, "OK, Ms Walters, you're it. Be aware of your casual observers, and let's make those passes quick and clean."

I saw Tina and Eva walking past each other on the south side of the square; their palms brushed for a split second as the coin passed between them. "Well done," said Mr Solomon.

Zach tilted his head back, closed his eyes, and soaked in the sun as if he'd been coming to that gazebo his whole life.

"So what about you?" I asked, once the silence became too much. "Exactly where does the Blackthorne Institute call home?"

"Oh." He cocked an eyebrow. "That's classified."

I couldn't help myself: I got annoyed. "So you can sleep inside the walls of *my* school, but I can't even know where yours *is*?"

Zach laughed again, but it was different this time, not mocking but deeper, as if I were on the outside of a joke I could never hope to understand. "Trust me, Gallagher Girl, you wouldn't want to sleep in my school."

OK, I have to admit at that point my spy genetics and teenage curiosity were about to overwhelm me.

Through my comms unit, I heard Mr Solomon say, "Two men are playing chess in the southwest corner of the square. How many moves from checkmate is the man in the green cap, Ms Baxter?"

Bex replied "Six" without even breaking stride as she and Grant strolled along the opposite side of the street.

"What do you mean? Why can't you tell me?"

"Just trust me, Gallagher Girl." He straightened on the gazebo steps, placed his elbows on his knees, and something more substantial than a coin seemed to pass between us as he stared at me. "Can you trust me?"

A torn and faded movie ticket blew across the grass. Mr Solomon said, "Ms Morrison, you just passed three parked cars on Main Street; what were their licence plate numbers?" and Mick rattled off her response.

But Zach's gaze never left mine and I thought his question might have been the hardest of them all.

In the reflection of the pharmacy window I saw Eva drop the coin in the open bag at Courtney's feet while, through my comms unit, Mr Solomon warned, "There was an ATM behind you, Ms Alvarez. ATM equal cameras. Tighten it up, ladies."

Zach nodded and said, "Solomon's good." As if it didn't go without saying.

"Yeah. He is."

"They say you're good, too." And then, despite some very rigorous P&E training, I think a feather could have knocked me over, because A) I had no idea who "they" were or where they got their information. And B) Even if it was reliable intel, I never dreamed Zachary Goode, of all people, would say so.

"OK, Zach," Mr Solomon said. "Without turning around, tell me how many windows overlook the square from the west side."

"Fourteen." Zach didn't miss a beat. His eyes didn't leave me for a second. Then to me he said, "They say you're a real pavement artist."

Zach leaned back on the steps again. "You know, it's probably a good thing we got to tail you in Washington D.C. If you'd been following me, I probably never would have seen you."

It was supposed to be a compliment – I know it was. After all, for a spy, there's probably no higher praise. But right then, as I stood in the place where I'd had my first date – my first kiss – I didn't hear it as a spy; I heard it as a girl. And for a girl, having a boy like Zach Goode tell you that he would never notice you isn't a compliment. At all.

I should have said something sassy. I should have made a joke. I should have done anything but turn around and walk away from the gazebo and my partner and my mission. Bex and Grant veered onto the pavement and headed straight towards me. I felt Bex bump into me, heard her say "I'm sorry" as her hand slid softly over my own.

"Nice pass, Ms Baxter," Mr Solomon said as I held the coin in my palm.

I turned down a side street on the far side of the square, passed the pharmacy, and thought for a second about the one boy who had seen me – once – and I wondered if life were just a series of brush passes – things come and go.

Then I heard a familiar voice say, "Cammie, is that you?"

Then I realised that sometimes things come back.

Chapter 14

Josh.

Josh was standing in front of me. Josh was stepping closer. Josh was looking at me, smiling at me. "Hey, Cammie, I thought that was you."

Now, I know I'm new to this whole ex-girlfriend thing, but I'm pretty sure exes aren't supposed to talk to each other. In fact, I'm pretty sure exes are supposed to hide when they see each other, which totally sounded like a great idea to me, because, well, hiding's what I do best.

But Josh had seen me. Josh always saw me.

"Cammie?" Josh said again. "Are you okay?"

I honestly didn't have a clue how to answer, because, on the one hand, Josh was there – talking to me! On the other hand, I had broken up with him. And lied to him. And the last time I'd seen him he'd shown up during a

CoveOps exercise, driven a forklift through a wall, and had his memory modified, so *okay* wasn't necessarily the word the came to mind when describing how I felt right then.

Spies are good at multitasking – we observe and we process, we calculate and we lie, but I didn't think it was possible to feel so happy, scared, and generally awkward all at the same time, so I muttered, "Hi, Josh," and tried to keep my voice from cracking.

"What are you doing here?" Josh asked, then looked up and down the narrow street as if he were being followed (which, when you think about it, wasn't all that far-fetched).

"Oh, it's a...school thing." At the word *school*, he recoiled slightly. I looked down at the uniform that – until that moment – Josh had never seen me wear. "So, how have you been?"

"OK. How about you?"

"OK," I said, too, because, even though I could have told Josh a lot of things in a lot of different languages, the things I most wanted to say were the very things that neither the spy in me nor the girl in me could ever let him hear.

"So we're both OK," Josh said. He forced a smile. "Good for us."

Oh my gosh, could this moment be any more awkward, I thought – just as...you guessed it...*the moment got a lot more awkward.*

"Josh." The voice was soft and familiar. "Josh, your dad said he could..." The voice trailed off, and I saw one of Josh's oldest friends step out of the pharmacy's side door.

DeeDee's short blond hair did a little flippy thing where it stuck out of the bottom of her pink hat. Which matched her pink scarf. And her pink mittens. Pink was definitely DeeDee's signature colour. "Oh my gosh, Cammie! It's great to see you!" she exclaimed.

She paused and studied my uniform for a second, as if remembering that almost everything I'd told her last semester had been a lie. And then, despite everything, DeeDee hugged me.

"Hi, DeeDee," I said, forcing a smile. "It's really... good...to see you, too." And it would have been if I hadn't noticed something just then that had nothing to do with being a spy on a training op and everything to do with being an ex-girlfriend.

DeeDee and Josh were standing too straight and trying too hard not to touch. A panicked look passed between them that screamed, *We've been caught.* And, *Do you think she'll know?*

It didn't take a genius to look at them together – to know that Josh and DeeDee were no longer just friends.

Spies don't train so that we'll always know what to think; we train so that in times like this we don't have to think; so that our bodies will go on cruise control and do the right things for us. My mouth smiled. My lungs kept

128

breathing. I maintained cover, even when I heard Mr Solomon's voice in my ear saying, "OK, Ms Morgan, let's see you hand off."

"We're...I mean...I'm..." DeeDee corrected quickly, as if trying to hide the fact that in the past few weeks she'd lost her single-pronoun status. "I'm on the committee for the spring fling – it's a dance...and you know...kind of a big deal..." She was rambling, unsteadied, which is pretty common for people in deep cover for the first time. "And Josh is helping me get businesses to donate door prizes and stuff. For the fling. Next Friday night. And—"

She might have rambled on forever, and I might have let her, but then a voice echoed down the narrow street. "Cammie, there you are," Zach said as he strolled around the corner, stopped suddenly, and looked from Josh to DeeDee and finally at me. "I was wondering where you'd disappeared to," he said. Then he turned to the boy next to me, stretched out a hand, and said, "I'm Zach."

DeeDee looked at Zach then back to me, and smiled that all-American-girl smile of hers like this was the most superfun reunion ever!

But Josh didn't smile. He looked between Zach and me with the same kind of expression he used to have while doing his chemistry homework – as if the answer were right in front of him but he couldn't quite see it.

"Zach," I said as my Culture and Assimilation training kicked in, "this is DeeDee. And Josh. They're..." I started before I realised I had no idea how that sentence was supposed to end.

"We're friends of Cammie's," DeeDee said, saving me.

"Zach and I…" I started, but then somehow couldn't find the words to finish.

"I go to school with Cammie," Zach said, and I marvelled for a moment about how smoothly he had lied, before I realised it wasn't a lie at all.

"Really?" DeeDee looked confused. "I thought it was a girls' school?"

"Actually, my school's doing an exchange with Gallagher this term."

Then (and I swear I'm not making this stuff up) Zach slipped his hand into mine!

"Oh." DeeDee's eyes got wide as she looked at Zach, then at me, then at our joined hands. "That's really great!" She beamed, and since DeeDee is about the most unspylike girl I know, there wasn't a doubt in my mind she was happy for me.

I looked at Zach, trying to see him as DeeDee did. He was sort of tall, and his shoulders were pretty broad. I guess if you have to run into your ex-boyfriend and his new girlfriend, then there are probably worse kinds of cover. (I know, because my mom told me a story once about the Privolzhsky region of Russia and a very unfortunate hat.) But that didn't change the fact that I was finally with Josh again, but Josh…was with DeeDee. And

I was holding the wrong boy's hand.

"Cam," Zach said, and I realised it was the first time he'd actually called me by my name – not *Gallagher Girl*. It sounded...well...*different*. "The van's leaving in ten." He nodded at Josh and DeeDee. "It was nice meeting you."

"You too," DeeDee said, but Josh didn't make a sound as we watched Zach go. He'd already turned the corner by the dry cleaners before I realised he had taken the coin with him.

As little as I liked to admit it, Zachary Goode was officially *it*.

"Oh...well...I'll let you guys get back to your party plans," I said as I stepped away.

"You could come," Josh called after me. I stopped. "Next Friday. You know, the whole town's gonna be there. You could come if you want."

"And bring Zach," DeeDee hurried to add.

"That sounds like fun," I said, except, if you asked me, a party with Josh and DeeDee and Zach sounded like the kind of torture that had been outlawed by the Geneva Convention. But of course I couldn't say that. Of course I had to smile. And lie. Again.

PROS AND CONS TO BEING A SPY
WITH A BROKEN HEART:

PRO: Whenever you feel like punching someone, you can. As hard as you want. For credit.

CON: The person you punch may very well punch you back. Harder. (Especially if that person is Bex.)

PRO: High stone walls and state-of-the-art security greatly reduce the chance of seeing ex-boyfriend and his new girlfriend in tremendously awkward social settings.

CON: Advanced training means that your photographic memory is now so reliable that you'll never be able to forget the sight of the happy couple together.

PRO: You're perfectly capable of putting all your old love letters and ticket stubs into a burn bag and hiding it really, really well.

CON: Realising that, despite everything, you can't set the bag on fire. Not yet.

PRO: Knowing that, no matter what the operation, you can always count on your friends.

"We hate her," Bex proclaimed that night as the four of us walked downstairs for supper.

"No, guys, we don't *hate* DeeDee," I said.

"Of course *you* can't hate her – that would be petty," Liz said in the manner of someone who had given it a great deal of thought. "But *we* can totally hate her."

That sounded great in theory, except…well…DeeDee wasn't exactly easy to hate. I mean – she's the kind of person who dots her I's with little hearts (I know because we found a note from her in Josh's rubbish last semester), and she wears pink mittens and invites her boyfriend's ex-girlfriend to parties even though she totally doesn't have to. DeeDee was utterly un-hate-able. (And that's what I despised most of all.)

The corridors were virtually empty. Delicious aromas drifted from the Grand Hall as Macey McHenry placed one hand on the railing of the Grand Staircase, turned to me, and said, "We could hack into the Department of Motor Vehicles and set her up with a dozen unpaid parking tickets."

"Macey!" I cried.

"It might make you feel better," she rationalised. "It would make *me* feel better."

But I didn't think anything could make me feel better right then, especially when we reached the marble floor of the foyer and Bex said, "You *could* go to that party and show him what he's missing."

Really, going to that party was the last thing I needed, because A) I'd sort of promised under oath that I wouldn't sneak off the school grounds anymore. B) If I went I'd have to take Zach with me (like that was going to happen). And C) I didn't have a thing in my wardrobe that could possibly compete with pink mittens on the adorableness scale!

I was just getting ready to point out those simple facts when I really heard what Bex had said.

"Wait," I said. "How did you know about the party?"

"Cam," Bex said softly, "you were on comms."

Oh. My. Gosh.

As if it weren't bad enough that I'd just had one of the most traumatic and heartbreaking conversations of my young life – I'd had it while wearing a comms unit!

My classmates had heard everything…Mr Solomon had heard everything…*Dr Steve* had heard everything!

That had been my chance to redeem myself in front of the Blackthorne Boys, and I had frozen. I, Cammie the Chameleon, had been seen…by my ex-boyfriend…and his new girlfriend…and I had frozen.

It took all three of my roommates to drag me into the Grand Hall for supper. I barely managed to stay through dessert before slipping away. (Really, there's no reason to waste perfectly good crème brûlée.)

But then I found myself roaming dusty corridors that I know are rarely used, passing entrances to secret passageways and fighting the temptation to slip inside, until finally I was standing in a long, empty hall, staring at a tapestry of the Gallagher family tree, longing to ease behind it – to enter my all-time favourite secret passageway and disappear.

And I might have, too, if I hadn't heard a voice behind me.

"You know, I don't think I ever got the rest of my tour."

Zach. Zach was standing behind me. Zach was

halfway down the corridor watching me, and I don't know what was scarier, that I had been sloppy enough not to have heard him or that he was good enough not to have been heard.

"So what do you say, Gallagher Girl?" He walked towards me then hooked one finger behind the ancient tapestry and peeked behind it. "Is this when I get my Cammie Morgan no-passageway-too-secret, no-wall-too-high tour?"

"How do you know about…"

He pointed to himself and said, "Spy."

Zach cocked his head and placed one shoulder against the cold stone wall, and suddenly I became acutely aware of the fact that we were…

Alone.

"So," he said, "that was Jimmy?"

"Josh," I corrected.

"Whatever," Zach said, waving the detail away. "He's a cutie."

And…well…Josh is a cutie, but I highly doubted that Zach meant it seriously, so I just rolled my eyes. "What do you want, Zach? If you came to make fun, go ahead," I said, laying myself bare (or as bare as a girl can be in a government-approved school uniform). "Tease away."

He studied me for a long time, his face fighting a smile before saying, "Gee, you know, I would…but you just took the fun out of it."

"Sorry."

I took a quick step, but Zach blocked my path. "Hey," he whispered. "Why'd you freeze out there today?" Suddenly he wasn't the boy who had winked at me in D.C., and bore no resemblance to the guy who had sunned himself on the gazebo steps. So far I'd seen three different faces for Zachary Goode, and at the moment I didn't have a clue which was real and which was legend.

"I'm fine," I said. "I'm over it."

"No you aren't, Gallagher Girl. But you will be."

Walking to my mom's office on Sunday night, I couldn't help wondering when it was all going to get easier. Josh wasn't even my boyfriend anymore, yet my life was still full of boy-related drama. Hadn't I spent a good portion of my winter holiday trying to put those things behind me? But that was before I knew that I'd stink at countersurveillance – that the drama would follow me wherever I went.

A few minutes later Mom appeared in the doorway of her office. "How are you, kiddo?"

"Fine."

But one of the downsides of having a top government operative for a mom is that, most of the time, she knows when you're lying – even to yourself.

"No," Mom said. I heard the click of the door as it locked into place. "You're not."

I could have told her it was nothing; I might have

informed her that I was as fine as I could be, considering that Eva Alvarez had barged into our room at 6 am in the morning (on a *Sunday*) asking to borrow Macey's curling tongs. But my mom knew better, so I just walked over to the leather sofa, sank into the soft cushions, and said, "I saw Josh."

And my mom said, "I know."

Of course I knew she'd know, because – well, she is a spy, and my headmistress, and there was probably a tape of the whole ordeal floating around somewhere. (Note to self: find and destroy that tape.) But right then Rachel Morgan was looking at me not as a spy, but as a mom. Maybe that's why I had to look away.

She sank to the sofa beside me. "I know it may not seem like it, but this *is* a good thing, Cam. Seeing him was a good thing."

But it didn't *feel* like a good thing.

"The tea we gave Josh is quite effective, but sometimes certain triggers can cause people to remember the things we need them to forget. Josh has seen you. He's talked to you. We know that he doesn't remember following you on your CoveOps final. He has no recollection of coming back here and being debriefed. The Gallagher Academy is just an elite boarding school to him," my mom said. "Josh is no longer a security threat."

So now we knew that Josh would never know the truth.

I've been punched hard before, lots of times, by people who know what they're doing, but something about my mom's words made me lose my breath. I know it's crazy – me thinking that maybe one day Josh would dump DeeDee the Adorable and suddenly remember the truth about me and love me anyway. I know that was a crazy dream. But it was my dream. And a part of me hated to watch it die.

"I know this is hard, kiddo," Mom said one final time. "So that's why I thought you might like something to take your mind off it." And then Mom reached behind her desk and pulled out a large white box wrapped in a beautiful blue ribbon.

Well, obviously I'd had presents from my mom before – good presents (signed first editions of *A Spy's Guide to Underground Moscow* don't grow on trees, you know), but I had a feeling this present was different. I felt like there was some kind of string attached.

"Go ahead," Mom said. "I think it should fit."

I untied the ribbon and let it fall to the floor, took the top off the box, and peeled away the layers of tissue paper.

"It's a dress," I said, stating the obvious – except it wasn't *just* a dress. It was red...and floor-length...and strapless! And I know normal moms probably buy normal daughters strapless dresses all the time, for dances and proms and cello recitals and stuff, but the last time my mom had held a dress like that she'd been getting ready for a New Year's Eve party on board the yacht of a Middle Eastern arms dealer, so something about that dress felt...different.

"It's beautiful," I said.

Mom walked over to the microwave to pop in some frozen burritos. "I'm glad you like it. I thought it would look good on you."

Which, to tell you the truth, I sort of doubted, but I didn't think it was the right time to point that out.

"Uh, Mom..."

"I also thought it might come in handy in a week or so."

I sat there staring into the box, thinking that whatever was coming, it was big. It was important. And it required formal wear.

Chapter 15

The Gallagher Academy has prepared me well for a lot of things, but none of those things are red. Or strapless.

Maybe my mom had forgotten that I was the girl nobody sees – The Chameleon – and chameleons simply don't walk around in formal gowns with empire waists and long gauzy skirts that flow when you twirl. It was as if my mom didn't know that this dress was for someone who was definitely supposed to be seen.

"What's the matter, Gallagher Girl?" Zach asked as we left COW the next morning and started the walk to C&A. "You seem…jumpy."

Well, he would be jumpy too if he'd heard Bex's theory that a terrorist group was going to take over a prom and we were going to have to go undercover and stop it, but obviously I couldn't say that. And in a few minutes, after we'd settled into the Chippendale chairs of the Culture and Assimilation classroom, *no one* was saying *anything*.

"The all-school exam," Madame Dabney exclaimed as she stood in the centre of the room. Soft rays of early sunshine glowed around her, and her voice had taken on such a dreamy quality that I almost expected harps to start playing as she floated across the floor. "Ooh, ladies," she said, then rushed to add, "and gentlemen. In all my years of teaching at this fine institution, I have never had the opportunity to organise such an exciting educational experience."

Liz went still, and Eva and Tina tore their eyes from Grant's muscular forearms.

"This Friday evening, all students in grades eight through twelve will be invited to a formal examination." Madame Dabney waited for what she must have expected to be a standing ovation. "A ball, ladies and gentlemen," she explained when no one broke into applause. "There's going to be a ball!"

Tina gasped, and Liz's eyes went wide in a way that can only be induced by the combination of both tests *and* high heels; Jonas swallowed hard and turned the exact same shade of red as the dress that was hanging in my wardrobe – the dress I was going to have to wear...for an exam mark!

There had to be some kind of mistake, I thought.

Surely Bex was supposed to get that dress and I was supposed to get instructions on how to access the dusty, dirty, mice-infested ductwork of the Russian Embassy or something.

Mice I can handle. Strapless bras? Well let's just say, I'm the kind of girl who likes things sufficiently *strapped*.

"Tomorrow during this time, you will each be fitted for a gown." She beamed at the girls. "And dinner jackets," she said as she turned to the boys. "On Friday evening you will be asked to participate in a cumulative examination – a night that will encompass everything we teach. And you will be expected to dance".

At that point I'm pretty sure every other girl in the room heard "dance".

But I thought back to Bex's words as we'd stood in the deserted East Wing, and I, personally, heard "rematch".

There's something to be said for having Joe Solomon blindfold you and fly you to Washington D.C.; after all, the hard part about top-secret, clandestine missions isn't the shock or the fear or the helicopter turbulence. The hard part…is the waiting. And I know I wasn't the only Gallagher Girl to feel that way, because in the week following the ball announcement, there were so many rumours floating up and down our halls, even I could hardly keep them all straight.

For example:

Instead of having a comprehensive exam, like we'd been told, we were actually going to have to infiltrate a prom that was going to be taken over by terrorists. FALSE.

All the girls in the Eighth Grade class now hated Macey McHenry since all the boys in Eighth Grade were in love with her. TRUE.

Chef Louis was going to serve poisoned appetisers so that we would have to concoct antidotes. Or die. FALSE.

Thursday's P&E lesson centred on defensive positions that could give the term "kick pleat" an entirely new meaning. TRUE.

Body-waxing as a torture-slash-interrogation tactic is illegal under international law. FALSE. (But if the yells coming from Tina Walters's bathroom were any indication, it totally should be true.)

By Friday morning you couldn't walk down the hall without hearing at least a dozen conversations that involved hair pins (and *not* in the usual lock-picking and/or self-defence contexts). A part of me was a little concerned by the state of my sisterhood, but another part of me knew that half of a mission's success is determined before the mission even starts. Prep work matters. And, it turns out, that goes double for missions that involve formal wear.

"Will you hold still?" Macey demanded as she grabbed my jaw and held my head steady (because everyone knows eyeliner can be lethal in the wrong hands). But how could I possibly sit there as if my liquid liner were the most important thing in the world? We had less than an hour before the ball began, and that was time I could have been using to go over my chemistry textbook or my CoveOps notes. Didn't my best friends know that this was an *all-school* exam – that's *every* subject, and this was my big chance at redemption?

But no. I couldn't study at all, because Liz was doing really painful twisty things with my hair while Macey gave me a three-minute lecture on the state of my pores. Meanwhile, Bex was busy sewing one of Dr Fibs's bulletproof cups into her Wonderbra instead of the foam things it came with. And I couldn't help but think that spy stuff is hard. Girl stuff is hard. But I doubt there's anything harder than spy-girl stuff.

I didn't even want to think about what the boys were doing then, because…hello…I'd seen the dinner jackets hanging in the C&A classroom, and they were all black. And so were their shoes. And their ties. And every single boy from the Blackthorne Institute had hair not much longer than a buzz cut, so I seriously doubt they were going through this. Nothing in life…much less espionage…is fair.

It was nearly seven o'clock. Our room smelled like perfume and curling tongs that had been on too long. And down the hall, I heard Anna Fetterman yell, "Does this make me look fat?" even though she weighs one hundred and two pounds. It wasn't just another night at the

Gallagher Academy. This wasn't just another exam. And I, for one, wasn't ready. In a lot of ways.

"Can somebody zip me up?" Eva cried, running into the room as quickly as is possible for a five-foot-two-inch girl in three-inch heels. Tina appeared in our room and asked if we had any duct tape (and I highly suspect she needed it for a very nontraditional use).

Everything seemed brighter and louder, and I couldn't shake the feeling that we were getting ready to be tested in a lot of ways, so I pulled on the red dress. I knew it was time for me to stop hiding – even in my own room. I blocked out the fact that it was Friday night. And that two miles away, a different kind of school was getting ready for a very different kind of dance.

I started for the door and said, "It's time."

I never really knew how *uniform* our uniforms made us look until I stood at the top of the Grand Stairs, looking down into the foyer. Girls of every size, shape, and colour wore shimmering saris and elegant gowns. For the first time I saw what I had always known – that there's not a corner of the world we can't disappear inside.

"You look lovely, ladies." Madame Dabney stopped in front of us and turned to Professor Buckingham. "Oh, Patricia, don't they look lovely? I wish I'd brought my camera... Maybe I should go back... Wait." She stopped suddenly as if she'd just remembered something. "There's one in this brooch." And then she herded Bex and Macey together while she took a picture with the pin that held a gauzy silk scarf around her neck.

Everyone smiled. And I suppose we did look lovely. Bex's dress was long and black with a strappy back that totally showed off her muscles; Liz looked like the tooth fairy (but in a good way), in a soft pink gown with a full skirt. And Macey, of course, looked like a supermodel in her simple green gown and her hair in a ponytail. (I know – a ponytail? Unbelievable.)

The front doors opened, and I saw some guys from the maintenance department coming in, probably to help even out the male-to-female ratio a little bit. (Let me tell you, the Gallagher Academy maintenance department uniforms aren't nearly as flattering as dinner jackets.)

Three of the Eighth Grade boys pounced on Macey, begging her to save them dances, and then I heard a voice, low and strong behind me.

"Well," Zach said slowly, taking in everything – from the shoes I couldn't walk in, to the hairdo Bex and Macey had insisted on. Then he leaned back against the railing and crossed his arms. "You don't look hideous."

I was pretty sure that was supposed to be a compliment, but my understanding of boy dialect was still a little rusty, and Macey was nowhere to be found, so I had to wing it. "Ditto."

Oh my gosh, I thought. Is he smiling? Is he laughing?

146

Is it possible that Zach Goode and I just had a formally attired, preclandestine-mission moment?

And maybe we had, but I'll never know, because just then my heel caught on my hem, and it took every ounce of grace I could muster to avoid falling on my face and out of my dress (you know...the *strapless* one).

"Easy, Gallagher Girl," Zach said, taking my elbow in the way Madame Dabney had taught the boys the day before.

I pulled my arm away. "I am perfectly capable of walking down the stairs by myself." He'd obviously forgotten that I was also capable of throwing him down those stairs, but then Madame Dabney floated by. "A lady always gracefully accepts a gentleman's arm when offered, Cammie dear."

See – I totally didn't have a choice – not with Madame Dabney standing there taking pictures of us with her jewellery.

I accepted Zach's arm, and we walked down the stairs, towards the biggest (and...well...fanciest) test ever. But was Zach nervous? No. He was just smiling that same I-know-something-you-don't-know smile he'd first given me in the elevator in Washington D.C.

"Stop it."

"What?" he asked, sounding all innocent, which – I'm pretty sure – he isn't.

"You're enjoying this way too much. You're smirking."

We reached the foyer and turned towards the Grand Hall. "I got news for you, Gallagher Girl, if you're not enjoying this, you're in the wrong business."

And maybe he was right. After all, I'd never seen the Grand Hall look as grand as it did then. Small round tables sat at the edges of the room, covered with orchids and lilies and roses. A string quartet played Beethoven. Waiters carried trays of food almost too beautiful to eat. The room was nothing like a school and everything like a mansion – perfect and elegant, and I was just starting to feel like maybe it really was a party, like maybe putting on a red dress and dancing at a ball might actually be fun.

But that was before I saw Joe Solomon strolling towards us, a stack of files under one arm and a look on his face that was a very grim reminder that tonight was purely business. That was before I heard my CoveOps teacher say, "Hello, ladies and gentlemen. You all look very nice, but I'm afraid you aren't quite finished getting ready."

Can I just say that it's a really good thing Joe Solomon is an extremely skilled operative, because at that moment he should have been very concerned for his physical safety. After all, that is *not* a thing you should tell a group of girls who have been recently plucked, waxed, gelled, sprayed, and mascaraed.

"I'm afraid we didn't mention that tonight is something of a *masquerade* ball," he said, and then the panic began.

148

"But we haven't got masks or…disguises or—" Courtney started, before Mr Solomon cut her off.

"These are your disguises, Ms Bauer." Instead of masks, he handed us folders. "Cover legends, ladies and gentlemen. You have three minutes to memorise every piece of information within them."

Immediately, Liz's hand shot into the air.

Solomon smiled. "Even if you are *not* on the CoveOps track, Ms Sutton. Spies are the ultimate actors, ladies and gentlemen. It's the heart of what we do. So tonight your mission is simple: you will become somebody else."

It didn't feel like we were playing dress up anymore.

He started to walk away but then paused to say, "It's an exam, people. Culture, languages, observation… The real tests in these subjects don't have anything to do with words on a piece of paper. Tonight isn't about knowing the answers, ladies and gentlemen. It's about *living* them."

I pulled the folder with my name on it from the stack and found a driver's licence, a national insurance card, even an ID from the State Department – all with my picture and someone else's name.

I know I'd started this semester with a promise to be myself, but as I opened the folder in front of me, I saw that I wasn't going to be attending a ball in a red dress – Tiffany St. James, assistant to the undersecretary of the Interior was.

And that was maybe the most comforting thing I'd heard all day.

☠

Chapter 16

You've probably heard of cumulative exams before; but...well, that was a cumulative night. Every language we'd ever learned was being spoken simultaneously inside the Grand Hall; everywhere I turned I saw someone pretending to be from a country Mr Smith had lectured on. It was a virtual chorus of music and accents and clanking china. And I was starting to realise that having a legend is a whole lot easier when you're with people who don't know the truth.

I mean, Tiffany St. James, assistant to the undersecretary of the Interior, was supposed to be an excellent dancer, but as soon as I tried doing the foxtrot I felt the entire school staring at me. Of course it probably didn't help that our current boy-to-girl ratio meant I had to fox-trot with Dr Steve.

"Ms Morgan, you look just beautiful," Dr Steve told me, which was nice and all, but I knew I had to say, "I'm sorry. You must have me confused with someone else. My name is Tiffany St. James."

Dr Steve laughed. "Excellent, Ms Morgan…I mean, *Ms St. James.*" He shook his head in amazement. "Just excellent."

And if it weren't bad enough that the only person who had asked me – I mean, Tiffany – to dance was Dr Steve, then Zach waltzed by, laughing and glancing at me over Liz's shoulder, while she rattled off every single fact in her legend.

"And I was named after my grandmother… And I'm a Gemini…and a vegetarian…and…"

Zach laughed again and twirled Liz.

At that minute Josh and DeeDee were probably dancing in a gymnasium full of streamers, but I was in the Grand Hall of a mansion. I bet the Roseville Spring Fling had a DJ – maybe a local band – but I was listening to Mozart performed by four members of the New York Philharmonic (because that's their cover and all). I wondered when I would start feeling like Tiffany St. James, assistant to the undersecretary of the Interior, and stop feeling like a girl in a dress she totally couldn't pull off. (Also, I was seriously hoping Dr Steve wouldn't ask me to join him for the tango.)

Courtney Bauer's legend said that she was the princess

of a small European country, so every few minutes her royal highness would insist on dancing with Grant, who was supposed to be an infamous playboy who owed a great deal of money to the Russian mob, and therefore was hiding from Kim Lee, who was supposed to be the illegitimate daughter of a Russian mobster. (Which was quite unfortunate for Kim, because I know for a fact she'd been looking forward to dancing with Grant all week.)

I wondered if all dances have this kind of drama – if there's always this much riding on who gets to dance with whom.

On the dance floor, Bex was doing the tango with the security guard who always had a mouthful of bubble gum. An eighth grade boy had cornered Macey by the punch bowl and was trying to act all mature, saying, "So, do you want to go somewhere more private?"

"That depends, do you want to keep that hand?" Macey replied.

Every few minutes Mr Solomon would stop someone and ask something like, "There are four men in the room wearing handkerchiefs, name them." So I stayed on my toes – watching, listening. That's why I couldn't really help but notice that Zach was dancing with everyone. A lot. *Even my mom* (who was undercover as the First Lady of France).

I felt myself sinking further into the shadows of the party until I heard someone cry, "Tiffany, there you are!"

Another of our teachers, Mr Mosckowitz, came rushing towards me. But Mr M. is pretty new to the whole undercover thing, so he leaned towards me and said, "Cammie, I'm supposed to be your boss. I'm the undersecretary of the—"

"Yes, Mr Secretary," I said, before he got us both in trouble.

Madame Dabney strolled by with a clipboard. "Addresses undersecretary of Interior as Mr Secretary – check."

I resisted the temptation to tell him that his fake moustache was an excellent touch. Mr Mosckowitz smiled, and I remembered that he had spent most of his life locked up in the basement of the National Security Agency, cracking codes, and even the world's foremost authority on data encryption probably likes being somebody else sometimes.

"I say, Tiffany, did you get those memos I sent over?" he asked, trying to sound all bosslike – and it might have worked if he hadn't had some caviar stuck in his moustache.

"Yes, Mr Secretary. I did." I felt myself becoming Tiffany St. James, which, at the moment, was a whole lot better than being me – especially when Mr Mosckowitz asked, "So tell me, Tiffany, are you enjoying the party?"

"Tiffany is the *life* of the party," another voice chimed in.

That wasn't true – at all – but I couldn't exactly say so, because Zach was coming towards us, a glass in each hand.

"Excuse me, Mr Secretary," Zach said, offering Mr Mosckowitz a glass, "but I believe this is your drink."

Mr Mosckowitz twirled his fake moustache until it came off, then quickly stuck it back on. "Oh yes. It is!" He took the glass and leaned in to me. "It is my drink, isn't it?"

"Yes," I whispered back.

"Thank you, my good man," Mr Mosckowitz said to Zach, and I couldn't help but notice that the undersecretary had spontaneously become British. "Good show!"

Through the twinkling lights of the party I saw my mom standing next to a far wall. I wanted to smile and wave, but Tiffany St. James didn't know that beautiful woman. And something made me stand up straighter, listen harder, and wish we'd already covered lip-reading in CoveOps, because even though two dozen dancing couples stood between us, both the spy and the girl in me knew my mom was worried about something.

"Isn't that right, Tiffany?" Mr Mosckowitz asked, and it took me half a second to remember that he was talking to me.

"I wonder, Mr Secretary," Zach was saying to Mr Mosckowitz, "would you mind if I borrowed Tiffany for a moment?"

"Not at all," Mr Mosckowitz said, even though Tiffany... I mean, *I*...might have minded a great deal.

"They're playing our song." Zach put his drink on a passing tray, took my arm smoothly, and pulled me onto the floor.

The bad part about being in deep cover is that you have to like what your legend likes, eat what she eats. Since Tiffany St. James did, in fact, like dancing, there was no room to argue. I *had* to dance with Zach Goode (after all, a Gallagher Girl always has to be prepared to sacrifice for her country).

In my (very uncomfortable) heels, my eyes reached Zach at about neck level. His hand felt broad on my back, and he smelled, well, different from Dr Steve. (But in a really good way.)

"You know the undersecretary," Mr Mosckowitz was saying to Anna Fetterman as we danced past, "is really directly *under*...the secretary. So really I'm just like the secretary, but..."

"Under?" Anna guessed, but I think Mr Mosckowitz kind of missed the point, because he smiled.

"So tell me, Tiffany St. James," Zach said. "What does a girl like you do for fun?"

"I didn't tell you my name was Tiffany St. James," I said, hoping to catch him in a mistake. "How did you know?"

"Oh," he said, cocking an eyebrow, sounding exactly like the charming and debonair international art thief he was supposed to be. "I always make it a point to know the

155

names of" – he gripped me tighter – "beautiful women."

And then he dipped me. Yes – actual *dippage*. And he winked. Yes – actual *winkage*.

"Come on, Gallagher Girl" – he spun me out and smoothly back – "relax a little."

From the side of the room, Madame Dabney smiled and made a mark on her clipboard.

But at that moment I was capable of doing anything but relaxing...

"Hey." We stopped dancing, and Zach shook me slightly. His voice was different. His eyes were different. He wasn't his legend as he said, "Gallagher Girl? You okay?"

Actually very little was okay...

Because my bra – you know, the *strapless* one – had come undone.

And things were starting to slide.

Just hours before, I'd thought that the most humiliating thing in the world would be to encounter your ex-boyfriend and his new girlfriend... Then getting saved by a Blackthorne Boy... Then finding out that the entire sophomore CoveOps class and two teachers had heard the whole thing.

But I was wrong.

The most humiliating thing in the world would be to have all of those things happen and then have your bra mysteriously snap open while dancing with the aforementioned Blackthorne Boy!

I was one good twirl away from disaster, yet Zach still had a hold of my waist; he was still staring into my eyes.

"I gotta go," I blurted, pulling away.

"Ms Morgan!" Madame Dabney warned as she walked by.

"I mean," I said, turning back to Zach, "if you could excuse me for a moment." Zach didn't look like he wanted to excuse me – he looked like he honestly wanted to know what was wrong – but I just wanted to disappear and take my disobedient undergarment with me.

I started away again, but Zach held on to my hand.

"Thank you very much for the dance," I said, and pulled away.

I felt the bra slide another fraction of an inch with every step I took towards the doors. (The dress, thankfully, was staying right where it should.)

Liz came towards me and said, "Hello, I don't believe we've met. My name is Maggie McBrayer. I'm a vegetarian, and—"

"Not now, Liz," I whispered, and walked faster.

Near the doors I saw a group of Eighth Grade girls staring daggers at Macey, who Madame Dabney had forced to foxtrot with one of the eighth grade boys.

Mr Solomon stopped me and asked which of the guests would most likely be concealing firearms, and it seemed like forever before I was able to slip into the empty foyer and dart up the stairs.

"Can I help you, Ms Morgan?" Professor Buckingham asked as she appeared on the second floor.

"I just need to go up to my room for a minute, Professor," I said, starting to move around her. But despite her bad hip and arthritic fingers, she was still faster than a girl who was afraid that any sudden movements might send her bra out the bottom of her dress.

"Oh, I'm afraid I can't let you do that, Ms Morgan," she said, blocking my path. "The headmistress said that all students are to remain downstairs during the examination."

"But—"

"No exceptions, Ms Morgan," Buckingham warned me, and somehow I got the feeling that Patricia Buckingham was never the kind of operative to let a bra emergency stand in her way.

Well obviously Plan B was the bathroom just past the library, but halfway there I saw a door open, and Dr Steve started walking towards me.

"Oh, excellent, Ms Morgan...or shall I say *Ms St. James...*" he added with a wink. "I was hoping—"

But I didn't have time for an excellent chat with Dr Steve – not at all – because I could feel the bra making its way towards my waist. The Grand Hall doors stood open. Anyone could come walking out at any minute, so I blurted, "Sorry, Dr Steve, I've got to go do...something," and then I did the thing that I do best: I disappeared.

I went down a corridor that almost no one ever used and walked deep into the heart of the oldest part of the mansion.

The noise from the party grew faint as I ran; Beethoven gave way to the sound of my feet. I hurried down the old stone corridor, listening, looking, until the party was completely eclipsed by the thick stone walls and dense beams, and I was finally alone...I was *supposed* to be alone. But there was Zach, leaning against the wall, and for a second both of us just stood there, staring. A strange look crossed his face. "Hey, Gallagher Girl, I thought I'd find you here."

Which was a very bad thing, because A) He'd only looked a little surprised to see me there – which means I'm predictable; and trust me, for people in the clandestine services, predictability is a very bad thing. And B) I'm pretty sure the bra was only hanging on by a thread – literally! I think it was hooked on the waistband of my tights or something, because I could feel it swinging around my thighs. (Note to self: find out why the Gallagher Academy can manufacture raincoats that double as parachutes, but not a strapless bra that can make it through one covert evening.)

"What are you doing here?" I breathed.

"Looking for you."

"Why?" I asked, even though I was pretty sure he didn't know that I'd actually come there so I could take off my bra and stash it in the secret passageway behind the Gallagher family tapestry. Still, I felt like checking again.

"Because this is where you came the other day."

"Oh."

"I thought this might be where you come…when you're upset." He stepped closer and put his hands in his pockets, which is Body Language 101 for putting someone at ease, but everything about Zach Goode made me uneasy.

He was handsome. He was strong. And most of all, I knew that even though Josh might have been the boy who "saw" me, Zach knew where my favourite passageways were; Zach knew I was a pavement artist; Zach knew where I sat in class and what I ate in the Grand Hall and who my best friends in the world were. Zach "knew" me – or at least the version of me that Josh would never see.

And that was maybe the scariest thing of all. So scary that I temporarily forgot I wasn't just being cool standing there with my hand on my hip – that my hand actually served a very different purpose – so when Zach cocked his head and asked, "So what is it, Gallagher Girl?" I reached up to touch the cold stone wall.

And my bra landed on my feet.

But I didn't have time to panic or worry about how I was going to have to stand in that very spot for the rest of the semester (or at least until Zach walked away), because a siren pierced the air.

A mechanical voice and the words "CODE BLACK CODE BLACK CODE BLACK" sounded.

And then the lights went out.

Chapter 17

The sirens blared, piercing our ears, and the words "CODE BLACK CODE BLACK CODE BLACK" echoed, running together as they reverberated down the long stone hall.

Beside me, the tapestry that bore the Gallagher family tree was moving, sliding slowly between a gap in the stones that then sealed itself as if it had never been there at all.

The only light in the corridor was the moonlight that shone through stained glass windows, but even that was disappearing as thick steel doors slid over them.

Although normal protocol says that students are supposed to report to their common rooms in the event of a Code Black, nothing about that night seemed normal at all, so I grabbed Zach's hand and started running towards the Grand Hall as quickly as my high heels would allow.

When we passed the recycling bins at the end of the hall, a container marked BURN – CLASSIFIED MATERIALS ONLY burst into flames.

The vending machines that double as secret entrances to the science labs sank into the floor and were covered with stones identical to the ones that lined the corridor.

And then, one by one, a series of lanterns that hung almost unnoticed along the corridor sprang to life, their pale yellow glow filling the darkness.

"I thought those were for decoration," Zach yelled through the pulsing sirens.

"If everything goes right, they are."

"So this means…"

Formally attired men and women from the maintenance and security departments ran past us, but didn't stop.

"Something is seriously not right."

Bookcases slid into walls, doors swung closed, locks slid into place, and I struggled to yell over the sirens.

"It's security protocol," I said. "There must have been a breach. The whole system goes into lockdown – nothing gets in."

Then, as if to prove my point, steel doors fell from the crown moulding, sealing the hallway behind us. "And nothing gets out."

As we ran past the library, I noticed movement through the glass panes and saw that the bookshelves, the

163

sofas – *the entire room* – was spinning, sinking, spiralling into the floor, disappearing before my very eyes.

"Does this happen a lot?" he asked, and the answer was maybe the most terrifying thing of all.

"No."

When we reached the foyer I saw that the front doors had been covered with the kind of metal used on space shuttles and nuclear missile silos. Emergency lights burned in the rafters, casting an eerie red glow over the place I knew well but barely recognised.

I rushed towards the doors of the Grand Hall, but then the sirens stopped. Silence filled my school like a tomb.

The doors to the Grand Hall suddenly swept open, and a hundred pairs of eyes and at least a dozen very powerful flashlights pointed right at me. I squinted and shielded my face against the glare. And that's when I realised that Zach was no longer holding my hand. I glanced behind me, but he was gone.

"Ms Morgan," Buckingham exclaimed when she saw me standing alone in the dark, deserted foyer. "Exactly *where* have you been? There is an exam taking place, Ms Morgan – not to mention a Level Four security infraction. Now, *why* weren't you in the Grand Hall with your classmates?"

But before I could answer, I heard a voice call, "Cameron!" I looked to the balcony overhead to see my mom staring down. "Come up here. Now!"

*

The Gallagher Academy is protected by lots of things: Our walls. Our legends. And some very impressive electrical gadgets that block any and all electronic frequencies from penetrating our air space. But that night, something – or someone – had tried to get in. Or tried to get out. So it wasn't any wonder my legs felt a little unsteady as I started up the stairs.

Professor Dabney stood at the top of the stairs, shining a light on the second-storey landing, and one look at her stern expression was enough to tell me that this was no drill.

I turned into the Hall of History, where I had seen display cases spin around and disguise themselves for the benefit of strangers: but that night they weren't hidden – they were locked behind reinforced steel doors; walls had swallowed shelves whole, and Gillian Gallagher's sword had sunk into a vault, protected, secure in its place as our most precious treasure. It was a side of my school I'd never seen, and even though I had always known that a Code Red protects us from strangers, and a Code Black protects us from enemies, the difference had never seemed so big until then.

"Cameron," my mom called from her office doorway – not Cam, not Cammie, not sweetheart or sweetie or honey or... Well, you get the picture. We were in full-name territory, and personally, I was starting to wish the big, honking sirens would come back.

"Mom, I didn't do anything!"

But instead of a show of motherly support, Mom stepped aside and said, "Come in."

Her bookshelves had been sealed with titanium shutters, her filing cabinets had disappeared into the floor, and in the corner her burn box was still smoking, but I couldn't look away from my mom, because the expression on her face wasn't disappointment or anger, but something no girl ever wants to see on her super-spy mom's face: fear. She sat behind her desk, more headmistress than mom now.

"What happened?" I heard the panic in my own voice. "What's going on?" I asked.

"You left the Grand Hall tonight?" The voice behind me made me jump, and I turned to see Mr Solomon leaning against the bookcases behind me, arms crossed just like I'd seen him do a hundred times in class. Somehow, though, I felt I was about to hear a very different type of lecture.

"I didn't do anything," I said again, because even though I've been behind my share of Gallagher Academy security infractions, I have never managed anything greater than a Level Two. (I know – Liz hacked into my student file and told me.)

"Cammie," Mom said calmly. "I need to know why you left the Grand Hall tonight."

OK, it's one thing to tell your mom about undergarment emergencies, but it's quite another to share them with your teacher – especially a teacher like Joe Solomon, so I shrugged and said, "I...uh...had a clothing...malfunction."

"Oh," Mom said, nodding.

"And you left the Grand Hall?" Mr Solomon asked, not stopping to ask *which* article of clothing. "Where did you go? Who did you see?"

"Mom," I pleaded as I searched her eyes through the glow of the emergency lights that filled her office, "what's this all about?"

But Mom didn't answer.

"Did you try to leave the mansion tonight, Ms Morgan?" Mr Solomon demanded.

"No," I said.

"Cam," Mom said. "You won't be in trouble, but we need to know the truth."

"No!" I exclaimed again. "I didn't leave. Something happened to my dress, and I left for a second, and then..." But they already knew about the sirens and the lights, and for some reason I couldn't bring myself to remind them. "What's going on?" I asked one final time.

Mom and Mr Solomon looked at each other, then my mom got up and sat next to me on the leather sofa, pulled me down beside her, and said, "Cammie, do you know what's in this mansion?"

For a second I thought it must be a trick question, but then I remembered what the mansion contained...the experiments, the prototypes, the mission summaries, and...most of all...the names and traces of every Gallagher Girl who had ever lived.

"Do you have any idea what would happen if the general population – much less our enemies – had access to what is contained within these walls?" my mom asked. I seriously didn't want to think about the answer. And the truth was, I didn't know the answer – no one did. And the most important thing in the world was that we kept it that way.

"Ms Morgan, you were in the halls tonight prior to the security breach," Mr Solomon stated. "We need you to tell us *exactly* what you saw and heard."

I could have asked what was going on – who they suspected and why – but when you've lived your whole life on a need-to-know basis, you eventually stop asking the questions that you know no one will answer.

So I sat on the leather sofa in my mom's office knowing that more was riding on my memory than it had for any test I'd ever taken. I closed my eyes and told the story straight through – from Zach's dance to the doors swinging open. I left nothing out.

"You saw Zach?" Mr Solomon asked.

"Yeah. He was waiting for me. You should ask him if he saw or heard anything," I said, but my mom's

168

gaze never left Mr Solomon's. "Mom…" I started, but my voice cracked.

"Everything's fine, sweetie, don't worry." She smiled at me and rubbed my back. Rachel Morgan is probably the best spy I have ever known, so when she stood and opened the door and said, "The mansion's secure, it was probably just a false alarm," I tried to believe her. When she hugged me goodnight, I tried to wipe the worry from my mind.

But then I risked a backwards glance at my teacher, who had removed his jacket and loosened his tie, and I couldn't help but think that the party was officially over.

After I left my mom's office I made my way through the red glow of the emergency lights. The halls were empty. The windows were covered. I expected to see running girls, to hear debriefs and a thousand crazy theories, but the halls echoed with silence as I slowly pushed my bedroom door open.

It seemed to take forever for Bex to say, "What did your mom want?"

Sure, they'd all traded their ball gowns for flannel pyjamas, but one look at my roommates told me they were anything but comfortable.

"She wanted to know where I was and what I saw." I kicked off my tight shoes and felt my feet instantly swell up to twice their normal size.

"Well…" Bex said slowly. "Where were you?"

And then I told the story – the whole story. Again. And when I was finished, two things were clear. A) I seriously needed to remember to go pick up that bra from the floor first thing tomorrow morning. And B) My roommates had been expecting a very different story.

Liz sat up straighter on her bed. "So you didn't decide to sneak out and go see Josh at the spring fling?"

"No!" I said. "It wasn't me! You guys know I wouldn't breach security like that."

"Of course it wasn't you," Bex huffed. "You wouldn't get *caught*."

OK, so it wasn't exactly the vote of confidence I'd been hoping for, but it was a start.

"And besides, you'd never leave in the middle of a test," Liz added. "So you aren't in any trouble?"

"No."

"And Zach just disappeared?" Macey asked. "He didn't even go with you to your mom's office?"

"No."

"Cam," Liz said, and for the first time tonight, I could detect fear in her voice, "what do you think happened?"

Despite all my training, experience, and instincts, all I could do was crawl into bed, pull the covers tightly around me, and admit, "I don't know."

And then the lights came on.

Chapter 18

I've had some very challenging days since coming to the Gallagher Academy (like the time our archery midterm exam happened to fall on nondominant hand day, for example), but the day that followed the ball was the most difficult yet – for a lot of reasons:

- Even though it was Saturday, no one slept in, so that meant girls were walking up and down the halls, talking in front of our door by 7 am.

- Even if it hadn't been for all the noise, I still probably wouldn't have been able to sleep.

- The kitchen staff had gone to such extremes the night before that our only option for breakfast was cereal.

- Extensive ball preparations during the previous week meant that everyone was behind on their homework.

- My elaborate, twisty updo from the night before made the hair-washing and detangling process very difficult and painful.

- Even though the teachers were busy passing along the *official* story that the Code Black had been a false alarm due to faulty wiring – the *unofficial* story was about…me.

The lights were on. The steel shutters had disappeared, and everything in the mansion was back to where it always was, but as soon as I stepped into the library, I knew things were different. The weird thing wasn't that fifteen teenage girls were in there at 9 am on a Saturday morning. The weird thing was that as soon as I walked in, everyone stopped talking.

Even Tina Walters dropped her book and gaped at me as I walked past the fireplace on my way to the section of the library devoted to world currencies (we had a paper due for Mr Smith). I ran my hand across the spines of books, looking, until I heard a whisper filter through the shelves.

"Well, of course they're going to *say* it was a false alarm," said a voice I didn't recognise.

I froze.

"Obviously her mom is going to cover for her."

And my heart stopped. "It's not like it's the first time, either."

I'm used to people talking about me...sort of. I mean, I *am* the headmistress's daughter, and my chameleon-ness is rather legendary, *and* my secret boyfriend had followed me to my CoveOps final and driven a forklift through a wall. So you could say I've never been entirely under the radar. But none of those things were ever followed by pulsing sirens and spinning bookshelves and a mansion-wide lockdown three times more secure than what would happen to the White House in the event of a nuclear war.

By lunchtime it was all I could do to maintain a brave, unguilty-looking face as I sat in the Grand Hall, feeling entirely unchameleony.

I couldn't blame them, entirely. After all, my ex-boyfriend *had* invited me to a party in Roseville. I have, on occasion, violated school security to see that particular boyfriend. So it shouldn't have come as a total surprise that, as I sat in the Grand Hall at lunch that day, eating my lasagne, the entire school was staring...at me.

"How did this happen?" I whispered to my friends.

"Well, everyone knows you used to sneak out to see Josh; and they know he invited you to a party," Liz said, not really getting the whole rhetorical question thing. (Liz likes questions too much to ever let one go unanswered.)

"And then there was a security breach, and the next thing we knew, you were there – looking…"

"Guilty," Bex said, summing the night up nicely.

"Cam," Liz said, leaning closer. "It's not so bad. No one thinks you did it on purpose."

Bex shrugged. "But everyone does think you did it."

There have been Gallagher Girl traitors before, but no one ever talks about them. Very few people even know their names. But right then I felt like one of them – or at least like people thought I was one of them.

"So, Cammie," Tina said, taking a seat beside me, "is it true that you weren't actually sneaking out to see Josh—"

"That's right, Tina, I wasn't," I said, kind of relieved to get it off my chest. Tina didn't even seem to hear me, though, because she just ploughed on.

"Because according to my sources, instead of going to that dance in town, you were really sneaking out to participate in a rogue mission for the CIA."

"Tina! Of course I wasn't."

"Really?"

"No, Tina. I wasn't sneaking out to go to the dance in Roseville; I wasn't sneaking out because the CIA needed me; *I wasn't sneaking out!*"

Tina rolled her eyes.

"Tina, I'm serious," I snapped. "You can ask my mom," I offered, but she didn't look terribly convinced. "You can ask Zach."

And this got her attention.

"You were with Zach?" she whispered. "You were with Zach!" Tina yelled, and then she was off to where the boys sat at the end of the long table.

I tried to pretend I wasn't watching, that I didn't care. But I was. And I did.

"So, Zach." Tina leaned over him while he ate. "Is it true that you were with Cammie last night during the Code Black?"

"Cammie?" Zach asked, sounding confused. "Morgan?" he asked again, then laughed. "Why would I be with *her*?"

I thought my throat was going to swell up. I thought my head was going to explode from all the anger and embarrassment that was sending blood to my cheeks. But that wasn't the worst part. The worst part was that Tina believed him. She took one look at Zach and then at me and seemed to know that a boy like Zach wouldn't be with a girl like me.

"Yeah, sure, I saw her at the party," Zach went on. Then he laughed that little half-laugh of his again. "But I wasn't *with* her."

The spy in me wanted to utilise some highly illegal interrogation tactics (or perhaps the whole-body-waxing thing) and force him to admit the truth. The girl in me…well…she just sat there, too stunned and embarrassed to do anything at all.

175

"Zach," I started, but he just got up and left the table.

"See ya later," he said, as if he barely saw me.

I could feel every eye turning towards me, and at that moment I was the least invisible Gallagher Girl in the room.

There are many things I love about the P&E barn, like the way the light filters through the skylight, and how sometimes in winter birds nest in the rafters and you can hear chirping and singing in between all the grunts and kicks. (I don't necessarily like the landing in bird poop part, but that's just another incentive to keep you on your feet.) That day, however, the thing I loved most about the P&E barn was that it's a place where you're allowed – even expected – *to hit people.*

"You liar!" I yelled as I walked into the barn. Light bathed the old timbers, and the whole room seemed to glow.

But Zach just stopped punching the heavy bag for a second and said, "Spy," as if that made everything all right. Which, let me tell you, it didn't.

First, there was the fact that he'd lied to a member of the sisterhood, and even though he technically isn't a sister, that is simply not done. Plus, there was the fact that he'd completely humiliated me in front of the entire school.

And then there was the thought that had haunted me all the way from the Grand Hall to the P&E barn. Either

Zach didn't want to admit to being alone with me, or he knew more about what had happened last night than he was willing to admit. At the moment I don't know which answer I preferred; all I really knew was that, in either case, Zachary Goode had something to hide.

His fists were sure and steady as they beat the heavy bag. Small beads of sweat ran down the side of his face and onto the mat beneath us.

"Zach!" I yelled as if maybe he'd forgotten I was there. "You *know* I didn't breach security last night. You know I didn't cause the Code Black."

He looked at me and said, "Oh, I thought it was a false alarm," in the manner of someone who didn't think it was a false alarm at all.

I hit the bag with all my might, and Zach raised his eyebrows. "Not bad." He stepped around to hold the bag. "Put your shoulder into it now."

"I know how to do it," I snapped.

"Do you?" he asked, smiling that same winking, mocking smile. And then, I don't know if it was nerves or PMS or just the fury of a woman scorned, but I hauled off and kicked the heavy bag – hard – and it flew back and hit him in the stomach. For a second he stood there, doubled over, trying to catch his breath. "Nice one, Gallagher Girl."

"Don't call me—"

"Look," Zach cut me off as he stepped around the bag and placed his hands on my shoulders. "Do you really want everyone knowing we were together?" He paused. "Do you think that maybe what happened last night isn't any of Tina Walters's business?"

Honestly, twenty-four hours earlier I would have hated the thought of Tina Walters thinking that Zach and I were off somewhere together, but everything looks different after you've seen the world go black.

"Besides," Zach said as he smiled and wiped sweat from his upper lip with the back of his hand, "I thought you liked your interludes secret and mysterious. Your boyfriends private."

"We weren't having an *interlude*. And you are *not* my boyfriend."

"Yeah." He hit the bag harder. "I noticed."

"What's that supposed to mean?"

Zach stopped. The bag swung back and forth, keeping time as he shook his head and said, "You're the Gallagher Girl. You figure it out."

Boys! Are they always this impossible? Do they always say cryptic, indecipherable things? (Note to self: work with Liz to adapt her boy-to-English translator into a more mobile form – like maybe a watch or necklace.)

"Besides," Zach said, "at my school, we learn how to keep a secret."

"Yeah. I know. I go to a school like yours."

He looked at me. "Do you?"

*

I've found a lot of secret passageways in my time as a Gallagher Girl. During my Seventh Grade year I was almost always covered in dust and cobwebs as I pulled levers and pushed stones until I unearthed a version of my school that probably hadn't been seen since Gilly herself had roamed our halls. But when I'd found the narrow tunnel that led to a hidden room outside my mom's office, I'd kind of made an unspoken promise to myself that I wouldn't use it – that I'd never eavesdrop. But that night felt like an exception.

Dust hung heavy in the tunnel. My shoulders grazed old stones and rough wooden beams. Light fell through gaps in the stones as the passageway widened, and soon I was looking for my mom through the cracks – but seeing Mr Solomon. "Do you think any of the girls have guessed?" he asked.

"About Blackthorne?" Mom asked, and Mr Solomon nodded.

"No. But if one of them knew the truth, then they'd all know the truth."

Mr Solomon laughed. "You're probably right." He straightened out on the sofa. "You still think this is a good idea?"

Mom walked to her desk. "It's what we have to do." She turned and looked into the distance. "For everyone."

On the way to our room I avoided the busy staircases and crowded hallways – not because of the stares and whispers, but because I wanted to think about the way Zach looked during the Code Black; I wanted to remember the long, quiet ride from Washington D.C. and my mom's worried face. And more than anything, I wanted to ask myself the question that had been looming in the back of my mind since I'd first seen Zach in Washington: Who were those boys, really?

All we had was a picture of Mr Solomon in a T-shirt and my mom's word that we needed to forge friendships for the future. That didn't change the fact that the Gallagher Academy hadn't had a Code Black since the end of the cold war – until *they* showed up. That didn't change the fact that Zach had looked Tina in the eye and lied.

Twenty-four hours before, I'd stood in that cold, empty corridor and thought that Zach knew me; but I didn't know him. I didn't know any of them. And I didn't like it. At all.

I pushed open the door to our room and announced to my roommates, "We've got work to do."

Chapter 19

I know what you're thinking. And the truth is, I might have thought it, too. I mean, it's not like we had a lot of free time on our hands and were looking for an extra project. It's not as if I enjoy getting summoned to Washington and debriefed by the CIA. I don't go looking for trouble, but I couldn't shake the feeling that trouble might have found us – walked through our front gates and moved into the East Wing. So even though there were about a million reasons to forget the whole thing...we didn't. Instead we waited, and we watched, and a week later we were ready. Sort of.

"Tell me again why this *isn't* an incredibly bad idea," I muttered in the dark passageway. Cobwebs clung to every inch of me. My equipment belt was on too tight, and Liz kept stepping on my heels and making high-pitched squeaks (everyone knows she's afraid of spiders).

"Well, I think it's bloody brilliant," Bex replied. It was also bloody risky, and that, I knew, was part of its appeal for Bex.

I hadn't meant for it to come down to this. Seriously. I thought we might look up their birth certificates or do other least-intrusive-means-necessary things. But as I stood in the secret passageway that led to the East Wing, I couldn't help but feel pretty intrusive.

"Guys, maybe breaking about a dozen rules isn't a good way to...you know...prove I didn't break any rules," I suggested.

But Bex just smiled through the dusty dim light. "It is if we don't get caught." She stepped over one of the thin motion-sensing lasers that the security department must have installed over the winter break. "And I don't plan on getting caught."

I stopped in the corridor, felt Liz, then Bex bang into me as I listened for something – anything – to give us an excuse to turn around.

"But what if they aren't really gone?" I asked.

"They are," Bex said.

"But shouldn't we wait? We've only had a week of prep work. We don't know their patterns of behaviour yet. We don't—"

"Cam, I told you," Liz said. "Dr Steve is making the boys do some kind of group-bonding thing. It *has* to be tonight."

And she was right, as usual – but that didn't make me feel better.

Summary of Surveillance
The Operatives undertook a high-risk operation that could lead to answers...or expulsion...or both.

"Don't worry, Cam," Bex whispered. "It's not *that* different from when we broke into Josh's house."

I crouched at the air vent that would take us into the boys' rooms and reached for the tiny bottle of hair spray that I keep for emergencies (just not of the hair variety) and sprayed the area around the grate. A grid of tiny motion detectors flickered in the fumes.

"Yeah," I whispered. "Just like Josh's."

Liz hooked a device up to the laser circuits, and I watched the red beams disappear. Then there was nothing standing between us and the forbidden wing – between us and possible answers.

But here's the thing about black bag jobs. 1) You don't actually have to carry a black bag to break and enter and obtain covert information (even though they do come in handy). And 2) No matter how clear your objectives, you're never one hundred per cent sure what you're looking for. After all, it might have been nice to find a file labelled TOP-SECRET PLAN TO INFILTRATE AND DESTROY THE GALLAGHER ACADEMY, but I would have settled for some clue about the boys who now shared our classes; I would have been happy with a snapshot that showed me the *real* Zach Goode.

As we slid through the vent and dropped to the floor of the common room, Bex said, "OK, Liz, start on the computers. Cam, you and I can…" But then she trailed off. She stopped and stared. The three of us had officially gone where no Gallagher Girl had ever been before, and standing there, I couldn't shake the feeling that nothing in our training had prepared us for…that.

We'd been to these rooms only weeks before, but everything seemed smaller now. Greener, too (but that's probably because we were wearing night-vision goggles). And…

"Oh. My. Gosh." For the first time I couldn't fault Bex for being overdramatic.

Moonlight fell through the windows. Someone had left a desk lamp shining in the corner of the room. I pulled off my goggles, letting my eyes adjust to the dim light as I looked around the room. Liz's hopes of scientifically analysing typical teen-boy behaviour was going to have to wait, because one look at this space was enough to tell us that these were not *typical* boys.

"Are all boys so…" Liz started, but couldn't seem to find the words to finish.

"Clean?" Bex suggested, sounding pretty disgusted, because (take it from someone who has lived with her for four years) no one appreciates the "lived-in" look

184

more than Rebecca Baxter.

There were eight large rooms, where we found freshly shined shoes and beds made with hospital corners. Books and notebooks were stacked neatly on desks. There were no socks on the floor; no girlie calendars or back issues of *Sports Illustrated*. It seemed more like the barracks of soldiers than the rooms of boys, and I instantly regretted leaving Macey outside to serve as our lookout, because if we'd ever needed the Gallagher Academy's resident boy expert, that was the time.

Everything was temporary. And sterile. And with every step I felt more sure that the Blackthorne Boys were simply passing through. Which was both a little comforting – and a lot confusing. Why were they here?

Liz settled herself at the first computer she saw, pulled a disk from her pocket, and started uploading a spyware file that the National Security Agency has been trying to buy from her for years. "One-hundred-and-sixteen-bit encryption?" she said, sounding shocked and a little disappointed when she reached the machine's firewall.

"Maybe they'll challenge you next time, sweetheart," Bex said as she ran to the first bathroom she saw, pulled a pair of tweezers from her utility belt, and started yanking bristles out of toothbrushes for DNA analysis (just in case the boys were really biologically engineered spying machines or something). I stared at the empty walls and the barren desks, looking for family pictures or letters from home – the things that, more than fingerprints and DNA, would tell us who these boys really were.

As I looked in the first wardrobe, something dawned on me. "These trousers are brand new," I said. "So are the shoes." I thought about my own wardrobe – half of my school shirts had indiscreet stains somewhere on the white collars. My pullovers were all comfy and well-worn. I turned to Bex. "What are the odds that fifteen boys – all different ages – got their uniforms at the same time?"

She shrugged then fumbled in her bag for a pair of very tiny wires attached to small glass orbs, exactly the size and shape of the plastic buttons present in the Gallagher Academy smoke detectors.

"Bex," I cried, "we can't put cameras in their bedrooms."

"But a picture is worth a thousand words," she said, feigning innocence.

"Bugs only," I warned, because while I may be a highly inquisitive future government operative, I wasn't willing to go that far for my cause – yet.

"Fine," she sighed, putting the cameras back and retrieving the teeny tiny microphones that had bought me an A-minus on my freshman final. (They're currently being used by the Department of Homeland Security.)

There really is an art to planting bugs. Sadly, Mr Solomon hadn't covered it yet, but we did all the obvious stuff like put trackers in their shoes and dust for prints. You know – the basics. Not even Dr Steve's room – or

186

shoes – were immune from our artistry. (Note to self: never volunteer to investigate Dr Steve's underwear drawer ever again!) Ten minutes later I thought we were almost done; I walked down the passageway and Bex fed me wires through the electrical sockets.

I started back down the long, dusty corridor, wires trailing behind me as I made my way to our new observation post (aka the secret room I'd discovered during spring holidays of our freshman year). I was just starting to think that we might actually pull it off undetected, but then…I heard it.

"Oh, Ms McHenry, that is an excellent idea, simply excellent!"

Dr Steve. I could hear Dr Steve's voice through the heating vents, which meant he was in the hallway right outside. The hallway leading to the boys' rooms. The rooms that Bex and Liz were still inside!

"We've got to go, guys," I said. "Abort!" Then I remembered the massive jammers that block any and all signals within the Gallagher grounds – that we weren't wearing comms units and Bex and Liz couldn't hear me. They'd have no idea what was happening unless they'd heard Dr Steve and Macey in the hallway.

"But, Dr Steve," Macey practically yelled, "I was hoping I could talk to you for a few minutes."

"Not now, Ms McHenry," the man said. "I'm afraid I've only got a second to pop into my room before I get back to the boys."

I pressed against the bookshelf that serves as one of the entrances to the passageway and saw Dr Steve reach for the door while Macey tried to block his path.

"But I only need a minute," she said, whining like the spoiled brat she's supposed to be.

"Perhaps we can talk tomorrow, Ms McHenry," Dr Steve said, giving her a pat on the shoulder.

He was stepping towards the door. He was getting closer.

I couldn't take the chance, so I dropped my utility belt where I stood, pushed against the bookshelf, and stepped into the hallway behind the teacher.

"Hello, Dr Steve," I said. When he turned, Macey instantly stopped whining and gave me a "Is the coast clear?" look, but of course it wasn't.

"Oh, good," I said to Macey. "You found him."

This seemed to get the man's attention. "You ladies have been looking for me?"

"Actually, *I* have been looking for you."

"Yes," Macey said, catching on. "Cammie really needs to talk."

"So this is some sort of emergency?" Dr Steve nodded as if this confirmed some deep, dark psychological profile that he'd seen about me somewhere. (Note to self: find out if there is a deep, dark psychological profile about me.) "I see," he said, in the manner of a man who doesn't really see anything.

The Operative was able to neutralise the immediate threat to the operation by feigning severe mental distress – which was easier than she'd thought, since she was feeling both distressed and mental.

Unfortunately, it's one of the basic laws of physics (as well as espionage) that every action will have an equal and opposite reaction, and I realised too late that Dr Steve was expecting some kind of emergency. And I was going to have to give him one.

"So," I said, trying to sound as Bexlike and dramatic as possible. "I guess you know I have a broken heart."

Yes, it's true – I said that. Call it nerves or inadequate prep time, but for some reason that's the part of my soul I chose to bear to a man who insists we call him "Dr Steve."

"Well, broken hearts are very common at your age, Ms Morgan. Nothing to worry about there, I'm sure." He made another move towards the door, and I ran through all the ways of stopping him in my mind (nineteen), while Macey grabbed my arm.

"That's what I told her, Dr Steve." Macey stepped away from the doorway. "Thank you."

I started to protest, to hang back and buy a few more seconds, but Macey grasped my shoulders and spun me around to see Bex. And Liz. Both of them were smiling.

☠

Chapter 20

Summary of Surveillance
Operatives: Cameron Morgan, Elizabeth Sutton,
Rebecca Baxter, and Macey McHenry

In order to ascertain the nature of the Level Four
security infraction that led to the Code Black, The
Operatives undertook a routine reconnaissance
mission that brought them deep into foreign
territory (aka the East Wing) at which time they
observed the following:

The students of Blackthorne Institute (hereafter
referred to as The Subjects) have set up residence at
the Gallagher Academy for Exceptional Young Women.

Although nothing of an incriminating nature was
found, The Subjects do exhibit questionable taste in

leisure activity capacity, since a search of their residence revealed NO television and an excess of shoe polishing paraphernalia.

DNA analysis revealed that the subjects are, in fact, male and, apparently, are not the product of any sort of cloning experiment.

Fingerprint analysis, however, revealed that they are males who have no records in any governmental database – even the REALLY top secret ones. (Of course, neither do we.)

Known associates: The Subjects are presumed to associate with each other, as well as Dr Steven Sanders (aka "Dr Steve"), PhD.

If the whole spy thing doesn't work out, the students from Blackthorne will surely have futures in the housekeeping industry.

Analysis of the rubbish taken from the room revealed that The Subjects use entirely too much dental floss for fifteen teenage boys. (Are they possibly using it for clandestine purposes such as very thin, semitransparent rappelling cables?) Also, they totally don't recycle.

I'm not one hundred per cent sure, but I think many girls fantasise about being a fly on the wall of a boy's room. Well, let me tell you, the fantasy is seriously overrated. (And we've got 272 hours of audio surveillance to prove it.)

Other than the fact that we heard one of the Eighth Grade boys bragging that Macey had kissed him during the Code Black (a lie he seriously regretted during P&E), all we could do was wait. And watch. And remember that of all the qualities a good spy needs, the most important one is patience.

After all, it's easy to stay interested in a target when he's about to purchase some black market nuclear weapons. When he's going to the dentist? Not so much. So we listened to the boys debate about baseball players and types of sandwiches; we went to class, and we waited. After nearly two weeks of listening to wiretaps and testing DNA, we were back where we'd started. The only thing we knew was that the boys appeared to be ghosts, phantoms – smoke.

There was nothing we could do but trail the boys to CoveOps. Zach, Grant, and Jonas were walking twenty feet ahead of us as we left Madame Dabney's classroom and started downstairs. Liz blinked her eyes a few times and whispered, "They are real, aren't they? I didn't just dream them, right?"

"Oh, yeah," Bex said. "They're flesh and blood," she added, emphasising the word *flesh.*

"Just because Grant calls you the British Bombshell—"

"Liz!" I warned. "Shhh!"

She lowered her voice. "Why can't we find out

anything about them?" It wasn't just a matter of national security with Liz at that point. It was a matter of pride. Liz was a genius with a problem she couldn't solve.

And to tell you the truth, I couldn't understand it, either. After all, Liz can break any code; Bex can sweet talk anybody into anything; and I've been hiding in plain sight since I was old enough to walk: we are not without our covert ways!

But as Bex and I stopped at the elevator to Sublevel One and Liz started for the basement, I couldn't help but wonder how a school for boy spies can exist so covertly that even a group of girl spies can't find it.

"We have to do more," Bex whispered as the elevator opened into Sublevel One. "We have to go deeper!"

Before I could say a word, Mr Solomon came into our classroom. "Assets." He pushed up his shirtsleeves and walked to the board. "Define the term, Ms Alvarez."

"An asset is an individual recruited and utilised by an operative to gain covert information," Eva recited.

Our teacher acted like he hadn't heard her. His voice dropped. "Listen up and listen well," he said, as if a single person in the room was not paying attention to him. "The most important thing any of you will ever do is *make people trust you.* You will become someone you aren't in order to befriend someone you hate." He studied us all in turn.

"We develop assets, ladies and gentlemen. We find

people who have information that we want and then we take it," he continued. "Or persuade them to give it to us. We find traitors." He paused and stared. "We lie."

I wish I could say the sick feeling in my stomach was because I'd signed up for a lifetime of deception and betrayal. But none of that was as terrifying as the look on Bex's face as she turned to me and mouthed the words: *Phase Two.*

That night, the secret room changed from an ancient, deserted space into a modern observation post. Evapopaper lined the walls. The sound of boys filled the air as my roomates and I listened to the bugs in the East Wing and made lists of boys and classes and opportunities to "develop a plausible pretext for a relationship", which is pretty basic spy stuff. And maybe pretty basic girl stuff, too. So it would have been fine – it would have been good – if there hadn't been a line marked *Zach* right next to an arrow marked *Cammie.*

"Bex should do it. She's the better actress." I turned to Bex. "You're way better at cover legends than I am...and flirting...and—"

"I *am* doing it," Bex said. "I'm taking Grant." She pointed to the chart. "And that senior with the wavy hair. And..."

"But Zach's our leading suspect," I exclaimed. "Why do I have to get close to Zach?"

My three friends froze around me, and neither Bex nor Liz seemed to know what to say; but Macey just shrugged. "Because there are one hundred girls and fifteen boys at this school, and for some reason, that one keeps coming back to *you*." She raised an eyebrow. "You're the genius, Cam," she said. "You do the maths."

I thought about the elevator ride in Washington; the way Zach had volunteered me to be his guide; and finally, the way he'd looked when I'd found him in the corridor right before the world went black. Zach *did* keep coming back to me, and every good spy knows that there are no coincidences...only plans and missions and lies. "So," Bex went on, "either he's a rogue operative trying to use you for some clandestine purposes. Or—"

Liz cut her off. "He *likes* you!"

And immediately I started hoping that Zach's interest in me really was about rogue operatives and clandestine missions, because...well...clandestine missions I can handle.

The Operative waited until an opportune time (while leaving the tea room) to approach The Subject.

"Hey, Gallagher Girl," Zach said, then flashed me his signature I-know-something-you-don't-know smile. "What can I do for you?"

I looked deep within me. I summoned my inner

superspy. "Mr Smith says our midterm papers have to be a joint project. And my mom said that I should make an effort to 'embrace the collaborative nature of this exchange experience'," I said, as if I were quoting verbatim instead of making it up on the spot.

Zach raised his eyebrows. "And you want to embrace me?"

"Only in the academic sense. Look, do you want to do this project or not?"

I could feel the stares of the girls who passed us, which is one of the truly terrible things about being a spy: when people are looking and talking about you behind your back, you're kind of trained to notice.

"So?" I asked, feeling more in control again.

"Sure, Gallagher Girl." He started down the hallway, waiting until half the Eighth Grade class was between us before yelling, "It's a date!"

Chapter 21

I had a date! (Sort of.) With an enemy agent! (Kind of.) The girl in me was excited and terrified, but the spy in me knew this was my greatest undercover assignment yet.

There was a time not so long ago when I'd thought that maybe dating and lying to the sweetest, cutest, nicest boy in the world might have prepared me for a life of deception, but now I know I was wrong. Totally and completely wrong. Because it turns out, real spies don't make a life lying to the sweet boys. Nope. The real lying takes place with the other kind.

"She's got to look sexy," Liz said the next night as the four of us gathered in the room, getting me ready for my mission. Or date?

Oh my gosh – is it a date? I wondered. "*Is* it a date?" I asked out loud.

Macey shrugged. "Hard to say. Will there be food or entertainment?" I shook my head. "The winning of cuddly toys through competitive means?" Another shake. "Then probably not."

Liz, I noticed, was writing *everything* down. "But what if there's kissing?" she asked.

"Liz, there will be no kissing. Or hand holding. Or dancing – unless we're studying C&A, and then... There will be NO kissing!"

Liz looked a little confused, so Macey explained. "You can have dating without kissing, but kissing without dating is entirely different." Macey walked to the bed and started sorting through the nine million tops we'd already ruled out as "too dressy" or "too casual" or "too cleavage-dependent" (since I don't exactly have cleavage).

"She's ready!" Bex exclaimed, spinning me around.

Well, I didn't feel ready. With Josh I'd always felt nervous; with Zach I did, too, but in a *very* different way. I didn't even look ready, not the kind of ready I'd looked like with Josh. Then there'd been lip gloss and skirts and shoes that may not have been conducive to running four miles in the dark. Now I just looked like...me.

"No," I said. "This won't work. He's a spy. He'll figure out that I'm...spying."

"It's perfect, and no he won't," Macey said. She placed a lip brush in her mouth and circled me, surveying what she saw.

"But shouldn't I look…better?"

"Cam, he's seen you in P&E," Bex said, obviously referring to my tendency to be, shall we say, perspiration-challenged.

"And he's seen you totally dressed up," Liz added.

"What he hasn't seen," said Macey, positioning me in front of the mirror, "is casual Cammie."

I felt like Barbie's less-than-perfect friend.

"Everything about tonight has to seem normal, Cam," Bex warned, not seeing the irony in the amount of effort it took to achieve the look of utter effortlessness.

"She's right," Macey said. "Guys are like dogs – they can always tell when you're needy."

"Just remember your cover," Liz said, handing me my backpack.

"And remember to let him lead the conversation – see what he'll give you before you know what you'll have to take," Bex said, quoting one of Mr Solomon's best lectures.

"Right," I said, reminding myself that we were just going to be in the library. What kind of terrible things could happen in the library, for crying out loud?

"And, Cam," Macey called after me. "Be yourself."

No matter where I went that semester, I couldn't get away from those words: *be yourself.* But I could never be *all* of myself, especially then, because a solid twenty per cent of me wanted to spike Zach's morning orange juice with truth serum and be done with it. (Actually, that was Bex's idea, but we were saving it for an emergency.)

As I walked down the Grand Stairs I reminded myself that I shouldn't be nervous. I'd been on dates before – both real and of the study variety. And studying with Zach – not Josh – meant I wouldn't even have to hide the fact that I was doing PhD-level physics in the Tenth Grade. But as I entered the library and looked around for Zach, I couldn't fight the feeling that "myself" was one cover legend I didn't quite know how to be.

"Hello, Gallagher Girl." He'd claimed a table in the back of the library. The VERY back.

18:00 hours: The Operative met The Subject in a suspiciously remote location, indicating that he may have had more "date" and less "study" on his mind.
    – Analysis by Macey McHenry

Books covered the table. His school jacket hung over the back of his chair.

I sat down across from him. "So," I said, feeling my voice crack, "what should we start on?"

"I don't know," he said, but I got the distinct impression that he did know. A lot of things. Because, for starters, it was my scientific opinion that Zach was one of those people who used his intelligence to make sure no one knew exactly how intelligent he was (a tendency Macey tells me is common among boys with really sexy arms).

18:02 hours: The Operative became overwhelmed by the complete and utter silence at the table.

"Zach," I said, just to make sure my voice was still working. He looked at me. "So, I was thinking we could look at the impact of propaganda in third world economies?"

"That's what you were thinking?"

"Yes," I said, but he kept looking at me...I mean really looking at me. I wanted to be Tiffany St. James (even if it meant wearing the strapless dress). I wanted to be a home-schooled girl with a cat named Suzie. I wanted to be anyone but myself as I sat there feeling completely out of cover.

"So..." I tried again. "I guess we should outline the report and maybe summarise our notes and—"

"Gallagher Girl," Zach said, not waiting for me to finish a sentence that didn't have an end. "Is there something you want to ask me?"

"No," I lied, and then we both went back to our books.

18:14 hours: The Operative began to realise that the study date might actually consist of studying.

How long does it take for two people to find a comfortable silence? I don't know. One time I drove all the way to Omaha and back, about two days each way, with Grandpa Morgan, and he hardly said ten words. My dad and I used to spend Sundays on the living room floor, trading sections of the newspaper, and there was no noise except for the sound of turning pages. But sitting there – with Zach – was different.

"So—" I started, before realising I had no earthly idea what was supposed to come next.

He raised his eyebrows but not his head, and studied me with upturned eyes. "*So...*" his word dragged out longer than mine, filling that terrible void of noise.

"So what do you think of the Gallagher Academy?"

He tried to laugh, then seemed to think better of it at the last minute. "Oh. It's swell."

The Operative noticed that The Subject's use of the adjective "swell" was either intentional sarcasm or regional slang and noted to check it against the Gallagher Academy database.

I went back to my notebooks but couldn't read a single word. I used to think talking to a normal boy was hard. Turns out it's *nothing* compared to talking to a highly trained boy-spy who may or may not have been bred and raised by the US Government.

I was just starting to consider aborting the mission altogether when two eighth grade girls came running out of the stacks and stopped short, staring at me and Zach. Then they turned and dashed away, their giggles and whispers floating to me through the aisle.

"You handled that pretty well," Zach said with a subtle nod towards the gossip I inspired.

"Well, I've had some practice, I guess. Besides, sticks and stones," I said, and it was true. For a spy, it takes a lot more than giggles to hurt you.

I turned the page in my notebook and felt my eyes lose focus as I listened to the silence that seemed louder in Zach's presence.

"I gotta say," he said as he laced his hands behind his head and leaned back in his chair onto two legs, balancing. "I'm a little disappointed."

"Disappointed!" I cried.

He laughed. "Yeah, Gallagher Girl. I thought you had a reputation for being...proactive?"

Which was a nice way of putting it, I guess. "Yeah," I said, wishing I could figure out some way to turn the conversation back to him. "Well, what would *you* do if everyone thought you had breached security?"

He smiled and leaned forward. I heard the front legs of his chair land on the hardwood floor with a crack. "I'd probably find out everything I could about everyone who...was *new*?" he said, as if the words had come right off the top of his head. "Who maybe didn't have an alibi on the night of the ball? I might even try to get close to anyone I suspected," he said. He eased in closer. "I might even bug their rooms if I got the chance."

"Hahahahaha!" (Yeah, that's the sound of a highly trained secret agent forcing laughter.)

"But *you* wouldn't do any of that," he said, standing. "Would you, Gallagher Girl?"

"Of course I—"

Then Zach reached into his pocket and pulled out a small wire that I had last seen disappearing inside an electrical socket in the boys' rooms. He dropped the bug on the table, then leaned close to my ear and whispered, "I'm not all bad, Gallagher Girl."

He pulled his jacket from the back of the chair and turned to walk away. "Of course, I'm not all good, either."

I sat staring at the bug, thinking about what it meant, as Zach turned the corner and called, "Thanks for the date!"

"What's that supposed to mean?" Liz demanded, but I didn't know which part of my horrendous night she was referring to – the part where Zach had said he wasn't all good or all bad, or how he had routinely employed countersurveillance measures (a sign of the truly cautious and/or guilty), or that he'd thought we'd had a date! To tell you the truth, they all made me want to throw up.

Our observation post was dusty and cramped, so we sat

on the floor, surrounded by candy wrappers and half-eaten bags of microwave popcorn, notebooks, and charts; and the only thing that was clear was that no matter how much it seemed like *normal* boys played mind games – going to school with boys who have had actual classes on the subject is infinitely harder.

"So did he think it was a *real* date?" Liz asked Macey. "Because he didn't buy her anything. Or was it just a study date? Or did he see it as some kind of *date with destiny* or—"

"Shhh," Bex said, holding an earpiece to her ear. "We've got audio!" she said, bright eyes shining.

21:08 hours: Audio surveillance captured a conversation in which many of The Subjects agreed that Headmistress Morgan is a "smokin' babe", even though The Operatives know for a fact that Rachel Morgan opposes all forms of nicotine use.

"So he didn't get all the bugs?" Liz asked.

"Or he *left* some," I said, running through all the possible scenarios. "Maybe he wants us to keep listening so they can feed us false information. Or maybe he really did miss some bugs. Or maybe he left some in the other boys' rooms because he wants us to suspect them. Or maybe those other boys really did breach security, but Zach just can't say so because he's bound by some kind of freaky blood-oath-brotherhood pact that—"

"Cam!" Macey snapped, jerking me back to reality. (I fully admit the blood oath thing was a little out there, but the other options were totally viable.) "He gave you the bug either to show you he's on to you, or to mess with your head, and…it's working."

Spying is a game, and so is dating, I guess. It's all about strategy and playing to your strengths. People think espionage is all fun and games – that everything we do is cat and mouse, but that night I learned a CoveOps lesson as valuable as anything Joe Solomon had taught me. Real life in the clandestine services isn't cat and mouse – it's cat and cat.

Chapter 22

"Lies," Mr Solomon said the next morning as he walked into the classroom. "We tell them to our friends," he said. "We tell them to our enemies. And eventually...we tell them to ourselves." He turned to write on the board.

"A lie is typically accompanied by what physical symptoms, Ms Lee?" Mr Solomon prompted.

"Dilated pupils, increased pulse, and atypical mannerisms," Kim said as I racked my brain, trying to remember if any of those things had been true with Zach the night before. If anything he'd *ever* said had been true.

"Spies tell lies, ladies and gentlemen, but that's not what today is about. Today," Mr Solomon said, "is about how to spot them. Now, a seasoned operative will know how to control their pulse and voice, but for the purpose of today's lesson, I think these will come in handy."

He handed each of us something that looked like the mood rings Bex and Liz and I had bought in Roseville in Eighth Grade. "Dr Fibs has been kind enough to share these prototypes of a new portable voice-stress analyser he's developing," Solomon continued. "It's equipped with a microchip that will monitor a person's voice, and if they are lying, it will vibrate very softly, alerting the wearer to the lie."

The piece of plastic in my hands looked cheap – practically worthless – but like most things at the Gallagher Academy, there was a lot more to it than met the eye.

"You have to be close to your subject," Mr Solomon explained as he walked to Tina Walters's desk. "And the rings can be fooled, with training. For example, ask me a question, Ms Walters – any question."

Tina hesitated a second or two before exclaiming, "Do you have a girlfriend?"

Half the class giggled and the other sat silently in semi-horror. Joe Solomon bit back a smile and said, "No."

Tina's eyes were glued to the ring on her right hand as she said, "Nothing. It didn't do anything. So it's true?"

"Ask me again," Mr Solomon said.

"Do you have a girlfriend?"

This time Mr Solomon said, "Yes." A moment later Tina was shaking her hand like it had fallen asleep or something. "It's not broken, Ms Walters," Mr Solomon said knowingly. "It's just not as good at detecting lies as I am at telling them."

I couldn't help myself; I glanced at Zach, who caught me looking.

"Partner with the person across from you," Mr Solomon said, and an uneasy feeling settled in my stomach. "Watch their eyes, pay attention to their voice. And see if you can guess who's lying."

I know I'm not the first girl in history who'd ever had that mission, but I felt like there'd never been so much riding on it. "Oh," Zach said with a quick raise of his eyebrows, "this should be fun." I didn't need the ring on my finger to tell me he totally wasn't lying.

I started coming up with reasons I could be excused from the lecture, but no one had been exposed to plutonium since the mid-90s, so I was stuck. With Zach. And my fibbing ability was about to be tested more than it ever had been before.

"What is your name?" I asked, thinking back to that cold, sterile room beneath the mall in Washington and the way a professional had gone about looking for the truth.

"Zach," he said.

"What's your *full* name?"

"That's a pretty boring question, Gallagher Girl."

"Zach!"

"Yes, that's correct." He held up my right hand. "See – not lying."

"Where were you during the Code Black?"

Zach broke out into a broad smile. "That's better."

"Answer the—"

"I was with you," he said. "Remember?" Then he leaned on the desk between us. "My turn," he said, grinning like an idiot. "Did you have fun last night?"

"Zach, I really don't think that's what Mr Solomon is going for with this particular exercise."

"I'll take that as a yes," Zach said. "We should really do it again sometime."

I looked at the ring on my hand, but it didn't do a thing. He was telling the truth. But I still didn't know what it meant.

"Where are you from?" I asked.

"The Blackthorne Institute for Boys," he replied in a sing-song tune.

"What do your parents do?" I asked, and for the first time he didn't respond. He didn't smirk. He didn't joke.

He just straightened the notebook on his desk and asked, "What do you think they do?"

I could hear Tina Walters asking Grant, "So what's your idea of a perfect date?" On the far side of the room, Courtney wanted to know what Eva really thought of Courtney's new haircut, but none of it seemed funny or interesting or cool at the moment.

If the Gallagher Academy were to sell truth rings on the black market, every girl in America would line up to have one, but I didn't need the ring on my finger to tell me that Zach wasn't acting or lying or living out some legend then. There was a lot more to the story.

"They were CIA?" I whispered.

"Used to be."

But I didn't ask for details, because I knew they were classified; and I knew they were sad; and, most of all, now I knew Zach Goode was a little bit like me.

Chapter 23

It should have gone in the reports, of course. I should have told my friends. We'd been searching for weeks for any clue, any sign, that these boys had pasts and histories – that they even existed at all. For one brief moment I had seen the real Zach – no covers, no legends, no lies. But as I walked through the dim, quiet corridors on Sunday night, I carried Zach's secret with me. I couldn't bring myself to set it down.

"Hey, kiddo," Mom called when she heard me enter the office. Smoke and steam rose from a small electric skillet behind her desk while the microwave hummed. When she came to hug me, I saw that she was wearing thick wool socks that were far too big for her – Dad's socks. She had on an old fraying sweatshirt that was rolled up at the sleeves – Dad's sweatshirt. And even though I'd seen my mom in everything from ball gowns to business suits, I don't think I'd ever seen her look more beautiful.

"Tonight," Mom announced happily, "is taco night!" I had to wonder if that was the same woman who had sat in this very room while the world went black around us, shrouded in shadows and the red glow of emergency lights. I knew I would never know all my mom's legends.

"How are your classes?" she asked, as if she didn't know.

"Fine."

"How are the girls?" she asked, as if she never saw them.

"They're great. Macey's getting bumped up to the ninth grade science classe."

Mom smiled. "I know."

Everything was normal. Everything was good. Even the tacos looked halfway edible, but still I picked at my fingernails and shifted around on the sofa. I watched my mom, who had wrapped herself in the last traces of my father, and said, "How did you meet Dad?"

Mom stopped stirring whatever it was she'd taken from the microwave. She forced a smile. "What brought that on?"

I guess it was a pretty good question. After all, normal girls probably know their parents' story, but that's not necessarily true for spy girls – spy girls learn early that most things about their parents are classified.

Still, I couldn't stop. "Was it a mission? Did you meet when you were both working at Langley, or was it before that?" I felt myself running out of breath. "Did the Gallagher Academy do an exchange with Blackthorne then, too?"

Mom cocked her head and studied me as if I might be coming down with something. "What makes you think your father went to the Blackthorne Institute?"

I thought about the picture but lied. "I don't know. I guess I just…assumed. I mean, he did go there – didn't he?"

She looked down at the bowl and kept on stirring. "No, sweetie. He had friends who went there. He guest-lectured on occasion. But your dad grew up in Nebraska – you know that."

I did know that, but somehow in the last few months I'd started questioning everything I'd ever known.

"So how did you meet?" I asked again. "How did you know…" I said, biting back the one question I really wanted to know but couldn't ask: *How could you trust him?*

My stomach growled, but I didn't feel hungry.

"Someday I'll tell you the story, kiddo." My mom smiled and handed me a plate. "Just as soon as you have clearance."

I sat in the secret-room-slash-observation post for a long time that night, listening to the wire taps. Searching for some small clue.

It was well after midnight when I finally eased out of the corridor and stepped over the ashes of a fire that had gone out. I slipped through the massive opening of a stone fireplace (one of many entrances to that corridor), expecting silence, expecting darkness, expecting anything but the sound of Zach Goode saying, "So the tour is closed, huh?"

Which is why, spy training or not, I bolted upright too quickly and banged my head on the top of the fireplace.

"Ow!" I cried, clutching the back of my head. "What are *you* doing here?"

"Come on," he said, ignoring my question and gently feeling the back of my head where a bump was starting to form.

I tried to pull away, but he pushed harder, and even though I know he was The Subject and all, it's hard not to get a bit of a shiver down your spine when a cute boy is inches away with his hand in your hair.

"You'll live."

"You're being nice," I said, honestly shocked.

"Don't tell anyone." He crossed his arms and nodded at the stone wall from which I'd just mysteriously appeared. A smile grew on his lips as he said, "So…did your bugs hear anything interesting?"

21:00 hours: The Subject admitted to leaving some of The Operative's listening devices within the East

Wing. Or he tried to trick The Operative into admitting that there were remaining devices...Or The Subject was just making covert small talk. Or...

21:01 hours: The Operative couldn't help but remember how much easier it is talking to regular boys.

"What is it, Gallagher Girl?" He asked, sliding his hands into his pockets. "No snappy comebacks? Non-existent cat named Suzie got your tongue?"

"How do you know about Suzie?"

He pointed to himself once more and said, "Spy."

Moonlight fell through the windows, slicing between us. There were no sounds of squeaking floorboards and giggling girls, and I couldn't think of a single thing to say as I stood there drowning in the silence, struggling for breath while my head throbbed and Zach leaned closer. And closer. His hand reached towards my face, and for the second time that semester I froze.

His finger brushed a strand of my hair away from my eyes, but then he pulled back as if he'd felt a shock. His hands slid into his pockets. His gaze fell to the floor.

And it felt like we might have stood there forever, before he said, "Why don't you ask me about it? About them?" I felt my breath catch as Zach glanced back at me. "I'll tell you mine if you'll tell me yours."

I don't know what surprised me more – that someone had finally asked to hear what happened to my dad or that Zach's tough exterior was crumbling. He didn't cry or shake, but instead he stood so still that when I started to reach for him I pulled back, almost afraid to break whatever trance he'd fallen into. I remembered Grandpa Morgan's warnings that there are some wild things you're not supposed to touch.

"It was a mission."

I don't know why I said it. The words were foreign to me, and yet they slid so effortlessly from my mouth that they must have been back there, fully formed for years, waiting for that chance to slip free.

"Four years ago my dad went on a mission. He didn't come home. Nobody knows what...*happened.*"

Then Zach looked at me and said the words I've always known but never dared to utter: "Somebody knows."

And he was right – someone somewhere knew what had happened to my father, but I couldn't say so. There was something in the way Zach stood watching me. A silence stretched out between us; and even though we were inches away from each other, it felt like a thousand miles.

"What?" I asked. "What are you saying?"

"I'm saying somebody knows," Zach said, not snapping, but his voice was sharper – stronger. "I'm saying you shouldn't act like there aren't any answers just because you haven't taken the time to look for them."

"What am I supposed to do, Zach? I'm just—"

"Just a girl?" he questioned me. Then he shrugged and sighed. "I thought you were a Gallagher Girl."

Zach walked away, but I stood there for a long time, wondering if I should go to my mom; if I should go to my friends; but instead I slipped into the corridors I hadn't used in months, pushed my way through cobwebs and darkness, trying to walk away from the tears that burned hot down my cheeks, because maybe I didn't want to admit weakness; maybe I wanted to wallow in my solitude and grief.

Or maybe crying is like everything else we do – it's best if you don't get caught.

Chapter 24

The next two weeks were honestly two of the weirdest in my life – not for what happened, but for what *didn't* happen.

Zach didn't harass me. He didn't tease me. He didn't even call me *Gallagher Girl* and flash his cocky grin in my direction.

After a lifetime of being the girl nobody sees, I felt like I'd become a whole new type of invisible.

And then one day, as I was leaving the Grand Hall, I felt someone bump against me and I heard Zach say, "Sorry." Then we kept walking in opposite directions – him up the Grand Stairs and me outside.

I didn't notice the note in my pocket until I was already outside, standing in the light rain that seemed to never stop.

I didn't stop to marvel that he'd just pulled off the greatest brush pass I'd ever seen. I didn't run for the shelter of the barn.

Instead, I stood in the heavy wet air, looking at my name scrawled across a piece of Evapopaper. I opened the note and scanned the page, the words barely registering before the paper washed away in the rain.

Well, obviously the note was gone long before I found my friends and barricaded the door to our bedroom – which was a shame, because, if ever there was a piece of evidence that needed examining, *that* was it. But the note was gone. Lost. We couldn't analyse the handwriting or the intensity with which he'd held the pen. We had to go on words themselves and what little prior knowledge we had about the subject.

(Copy courtesy of Cameron Morgan)

So I hear we get to go to town this weekend. Want to catch a movie or something?

–Z

P.S. That is, if Jimmy doesn't mind.

Translation: This weekend might be a good chance for us to see each other outside our school in a social environment, free of competition. I do not view other boys as threats, and I enjoy making them seem insignificant by calling them the wrong names.

(*Translation by Macey McHenry*)

"Oh my gosh, Cam," Liz exclaimed. "He asked you out!"

"What does it mean?" I asked, turning to Macey, who plopped down on her bed and pulled off her nine-hundred-dollar shoes that she'd worn to the P&E barn and were now covered with mud.

"You mean besides the obvious he's-asking-you-to-the-movies part?" Macey asked.

"Yeah, besides that," I said, because it couldn't have been that easy. Spies never act without motivation, without a cause, and I didn't have a clue what Zach's ulterior motive might have been. I didn't know why he'd asked me in a note and not in person. I didn't have a clue what the significance was behind him not signing with his full name. We'd been studying boys for almost an entire academic year, and yet I didn't feel any closer to understanding a culture where people insult you, then tease you, ignore you for weeks, and *then* ask you to the movies!

"He's got to be up to something," I said finally. But my roommates just looked at each other like there was another explanation. "Don't you think he's up to something?"

The rain grew heavier outside, the wind howled, and finally Bex stood and strolled towards me. "Yes. He's definitely up to something."

I looked at Liz for confirmation, but she was busy entering Zach's words into the Boy-to-English translator that had finally made it to the prototype phase.

"And that's why," Macey said, smiling, "you've got to go."

Sure, if you're a Gallagher Girl and you spend all day every day inside the Gallagher grounds, then the thought of going to town – any town – starts to look pretty good. And going with a guy like Zach Goode looks even better.

But not if you're a Gallagher Girl who is actually engaging in what might be a deep cover honeypot scenario… Not if your best friends think this is the perfect opportunity to A) Try out Macey's new under-eye concealer that's legal only in Switzerland. And B) Practise the classic three-operative-surveillance scenario…

And most of all, not if you're a Gallagher Girl with an ex-boyfriend in that particular town.

Saturday morning we woke to sunny skies. Winter had gone away somehow, melted with the snow, and now a pale sunlight filtered through the windows. And I remembered what I'd agreed to do.

"I can't do this," I said, not really sure if I was talking about Zach or the push-up bra that Bex was insisting I wear (because push-up bras were invented for honeypot situations). "What if I let it slip that we're on to them? Or what if he drugs me and uses me to access the restricted portion of the science labs? Or what if…" I trailed off, thinking of the one question I couldn't bring myself to say: *What if I have fun?*

Instead, I asked the other question that had haunted me for days: "What if I see Josh?"

I'd spent months shrouded in the safety of our walls, knowing that as long as I didn't leave the grounds I'd never have to see Josh again – which is a luxury normal girls don't have when avoiding their ex-boyfriends.

"Relax, Cam," Bex said. "We'll be following you on comms – you'll have backup. And besides, what are the odds you'll even see Josh anyway?"

"One hundred and eighty-seven to one," Liz answered automatically. I might have looked at her like she was a little bit freaky (which she is – in a good way), but she shrugged and said, "What?" defensively. "If you factor in pedestrian traffic routes, population numbers, and patterns of behaviour, the answer is one hundred and eighty-seven to one."

But there was one thing not even Liz had learned how to quantify: fate. I knew I was tempting it. Again.

My stomach flipped. My fingers tingled. Every nerve in my body seemed to be alive – pulsing with a charge that felt nothing like I'd ever felt on dates; and nothing like I'd ever felt on missions – just nothing I'd ever felt.

Liz did my hair. Macey worked a miracle with my

makeup. And Bex was busy sewing a button camera onto my jacket. We had a plan. We had been training for this moment for years, but when my roommates started downstairs, I looked at myself in the mirror.

"It would be okay if you liked him, you know." Macey lingered in the open doorway. Behind her, the hall grew silent as girls headed out for the long walk into town.

I thought about the rules of covert operations: don't get emotionally involved in a subject; never lose perspective or control. Better spies than I have flouted those rules and ended up heartbroken...or worse. I glanced through the window at the barn, where we learn to shield our eyes and protect our kidneys – we dodge punches and take kicks.

But even the Gallagher Academy hadn't figured out a way to help us protect our hearts.

"I have eyeball," Bex said through my comms unit an hour later. Which was a comforting sound. So far, neither Zach nor I had said much of anything, because A) When we got downstairs there was a huge group of people waiting to walk to town (one of whom was Tina Walters). B) The wind was blowing, so I had to keep my head at a weird angle to keep my hair out of my face. And C) Even though I'd been on dates (and missions) before, I'd never done both at once.

And finally, it's kind of hard to talk when you walk two miles only to find yourself in the middle of the

Roseville, Virginia, Founders' Day parade. Yes, I said *parade*.

Both the spy and the girl in me knew I was supposed to be *saying* something – I was supposed to be *doing* something – but as soon as we turned onto Main Street I heard the blare of trumpets from the Pride of Roseville Marching Band; I saw church ladies selling brownies and raffle tickets for a chance to win a homemade quilt. The entire town of Roseville seemed to be either marching down the streets or filling the square.

"He looks good, Cam…I mean *Chameleon*," Liz hurried to correct her mistake. I glanced up and down the crowded streets and couldn't see my roommates anywhere, but there was some comfort in knowing they were there. "Cough if *you* think he looks good."

10:41 hours: The Operative couldn't help but notice that The Subject both looked and smelled REALLY good.

Zach did look good. He wasn't in his uniform. He'd put something in his hair so that it was messed up in all the right places. And I kept thinking that there had to be something nefarious going on – that there was no way this boy was on a real date with *me*.

"Hey, Chameleon, you know you *can* talk," Macey said through the comms units. "It is allowed."

But talking wasn't exactly easy, because I was with Zach....On a date-slash-honeypotting mission! I had a comms unit in my ear and a package of breath mints in my purse, and there was a 1/187 chance I would see my ex-boyfriend and his new girlfriend... I was dealing with a lot of issues!

"Do you want to do something?" I asked awkwardly, even though, technically, we were doing something.

"We could go to a movie," Zach said. "Or get something to eat."

"OK."

"Or we could just...walk," he suggested, and for the first time I wondered if he might be nervous, too.

"OK," I said again.

"Or we could have that clown over there paint our faces and then go rob the bank," he suggested, as if I wasn't really listening. But I didn't fall for it.

"No way. Last October they installed a Stockholm Series 360 – it'd take us at least forty-five minutes to crack it."

"Good to know." He laughed.

Suddenly I wanted to stop in the middle of the street and ask Zach why he'd asked me out. I wanted him to confess that I was being honeypotted, too. But when Zach reached for my hand and led me through crowded sidewalks, it didn't feel like the gesture of an operative on a mission. And then, more than anything, I wanted to stop hearing Macey's words, *It's okay for you to like him*, because sometimes not liking someone is easier.

A middle-aged man in a red jacket lingered in the centre of the square. Antique cars lined the street while men with big bellies kicked the tyres and sipped lemonade. We were only two miles away from school, but the Roseville town square felt like another world. The most dangerous thing I could see was a crowd of little girls in sparkly leotards pushing their way down the sidewalk. Zach pulled me around a corner and onto a quiet side street.

"So, plant any good bugs lately?" Zach asked.

A spark was in his eyes, but I couldn't laugh. I couldn't even speak. The silence pulsed between us like the beat of the retreating band.

"Just so you know, Gallagher Girl," he whispered softly, "I'm going to kiss you now."

For the first time in months I wasn't thinking about my mission or my cover or my friends.

I wasn't thinking.

His hands were warm on the back of my neck; his fingers laced through my hair, and he tilted his head as he moved in. I closed my eyes.

And I heard, "Oh my gosh! Cammie, is that you?"

Zach said a really bad word as he inched away from me. (But I doubt DeeDee noticed, because the bad word was in Farsi.) The noise coming from the square seemed louder than it had just seconds before, and I knew that whatever trance I'd been in was completely broken – the moment was totally over.

Zach had started to kiss me. *I had almost let Zach kiss me!*

"Hi, Cammie," DeeDee said. She hugged me and smiled at Zach. "I'm so glad you two are here!"

Josh stood five feet away, staring at me, but he didn't say hi. I've thrown enough punches in my life to know when someone is hurting.

I stepped away from Zach as if I could make Josh forget what he'd just seen, but then I noticed the reflection in the window behind me – Josh's reflection – and I knew that Zach must have seen him. Immediately, my mind raced with a thousand questions – was that why Zach had tried to kiss me? Why did Josh look so sad?

There were no fewer than twenty things I simply had to ask Macey McHenry! I started scanning the crowds, looking for my friends, but instead I saw a man across the street.

An ordinary man. I'd seen him buying brownies and looking under the bonnet of a Model T Ford.

But no one on the street was talking to him, and his shoes were too dressy for a parade. I remembered what my father used to say about counter surveillance: *Once is a stranger; twice is a coincidence; three times is a tail.*

And this made time number three.

As the four of us started down the pavement, I

couldn't shake the feeling that I needed backup for an entirely different reason. Josh and DeeDee walked a few steps ahead, so I whispered to Zach, "Hey, you're gonna think I'm crazy."

"A little late for that, Gallagher Girl." At the word *Gallagher,* two women on the pavement turned to give us the Gallagher Glare, but I didn't have time to worry about my school's reputation.

"You haven't seen anyone following us, have you?" I asked. Zach laughed.

"You mean besides your roommates?"

I rolled my eyes. "Yeah. Besides them."

"No. I haven't seen anyone on our tail. Why?"

"The guy. The blue jacket." DeeDee glanced back at me, so I altered my words. "Don't you think he's *toasty* in that heavy coat?" which is spy-slang for an operative who is about to get caught, but DeeDee didn't know that. Luckily, Zach did. He turned, casually taking in everything from the sight of the convertibles carrying the Founders' Day Princess and her court to the way DeeDee said hi to almost everyone we passed.

"What about him?" Zach asked.

"The jacket's reversible. Ten minutes ago he was wearing it the other way. Do you think a lot of regular guys in Roseville take the time to reverse their jackets?"

We stopped to look in a store window's wavy reflection.

"Look at that guy, Gallagher Girl," Zach whispered as the man bought a corn dog. "He's a mustard disaster looking for a place to happen. I bet you anything he's got a big stain on the other side."

It sounded like a good point – it felt like a good point, but then Zach laughed, and something...was strange. I knew it wasn't paranoia. I knew it was bigger than me and bigger than Roseville and bigger than any parade.

"Now what are you two chatting about?" DeeDee teased.

"Oh, Cammie was trying to convince me that I should recognise that guy in the blue jacket." Zach looked at me, and I knew the words were for me – not Dee Dee – as he said, "But I've never seen him before in my life."

And it would have been good news. I may have relaxed. But then I looked down at the ring I was wearing, felt the subtle vibration, and knew that he was lying.

Chapter 25

I'm not exactly proud of what came next, but Mr Solomon himself has told me that spies do bad things for good reasons, so I smiled, I gripped DeeDee's arm, and I used that unsuspecting girl for cover as I announced, "I've got to go to the bathroom!"

"I'll walk with you," Zach started, but I didn't let him finish.

"No," I said, smiling at DeeDee. "It's a girl thing."

As we pulled away from Josh and Zach, DeeDee giggled and wrapped her thin arm in mine. It probably seemed like fun to her – two girls setting off on their own down the crowded pavement. But I was entrenched in another kind of adventure as I scanned the crowds, looking for friends and enemies on the bustling square.

"We can go to the pharmacy," DeeDee yelled over the

roaring siren of a passing fire engine covered with cheerleaders – the end of the parade.

"What?" I asked.

"The pharmacy has bathrooms," she said again, and I nodded.

"OK, we'll go to the *pharmacy*," I repeated loudly, hoping my friends would hear.

Something was wrong – Zach was lying, and a man I'd never seen was stalking Gallagher Girls in Roseville. And that's the kind of thing that never happened before the Blackthorne Boys came to the Gallagher Academy and brought a Code Black with them.

"So, Cammie, I'm really glad I ran into you," DeeDee said, as if I had time for girl talk. "I was wondering if things are…you know…serious? With you and Zach? You guys seem happy."

Despite everything, I stopped and turned to her. Was I happy with Zach? Could I ever be happy with Zach? Two minutes before, I might have had a different answer to that question, but in a spy's life, two minutes is all it takes for the whole world to change.

"Cammie!" Bex was rushing towards me, waving. "Oh," she said with a quick glance at DeeDee. "Hi." Then she looked at me and rolled her eyes. "I just got a call on my mobile," she lied. "We've got to go back to school." She sounded disappointed – annoyed. Nothing in her tone reflected any of the panic I felt.

I looked back at DeeDee. "Sorry," I said, already stepping away. "I've got to—"

"OK," DeeDee said, but her usually bright smile seemed to fade. "Cammie," she called just as I started to turn, "I really hope you and Zach are happy."

Any other day I might have pondered that sentence for hours, dissected it with Macey, searched for hidden meaning in the words. Was that DeeDee's way of telling me that she and Josh weren't happy? Was I a threat to their seemingly perfect love? Or was DeeDee just the kind of person who wanted everyone to be as happy as she was?

If I'd been a normal girl I might have replayed every second of that day – my almost-kiss, the hurt look on Josh's face. But I wasn't a normal girl. As Zach himself had reminded me time and time again...*I* was a Gallagher Girl.

"We had two guys on us, too," Bex said as she fell into step beside me. I stopped in the street and turned to check behind us, but she rolled her eyes. "I said *had*." She shook her head. "I knew we couldn't trust boys who keep their rooms that clean. It's *not* natural!"

Liz was a half-step behind her, already out of breath. I looked around. "Where's Macey?"

"Telling as many girls as she can find about the tails," Bex answered.

"Wait! Cammie," Liz panted, "you can't just leave in the middle of your date! What if Zach gets worried about you? What if he thinks you've been kidnapped?" Then she gasped. "What if he thinks you don't like him?"

"Liz," I snapped, "protocol says that we're supposed to report any suspicious activity to the security department immediately! We were being tailed in Roseville!" The words felt heavy. "And Zach recognised one of them." I took a deep breath before I finished, "And he lied to me about it."

I remembered the expression on my mom's face as we'd sat in the red glow of the emergency lights during the Code Black. Someone or something had already threatened our school once this semester, so I didn't worry about Zach's feelings or what Madame Dabney would say about leaving a boy during the middle of a date. I didn't ask my friends if they knew the reasons why a boy might try to kiss a girl, and all the reasons a girl might let him.

We'd had a tail in Roseville – that was all that mattered. I felt my feet pounding the pavement. As we reached the mansion, I finally turned to see almost the entire sophomore class running down the lane behind me. "You were right," Courtney told us, swallowing hard, gasping for air. "We had a tail, too."

And whatever hope I'd had that I was wrong – that it was all some bizarre misunderstanding – vanished in the wind.

We pushed open the mansion's doors, and I immediately felt the silence that's usually reserved for the days before classes start and after they end, when I'm the only Gallagher Girl there to roam the halls.

"Mom!" I called, but my voice echoed in the empty corridors.

Courtney and Eva went into the Grand Hall. Mick and Tina started for the library. I headed for the Hall of History.

"Mom!" I called again, but my voice was swallowed by screeching sirens as the lights went out and the words "CODE BLACK CODE BLACK CODE BLACK" filled the air.

Gilly's sword disappeared into its impenetrable case, the bookshelves around us became vaults, and metal shutters covered the windows.

"Cammie!" Bex called over the sounds of the sirens and my raging thoughts. "Cammie, come on!"

My best friend took my hand and pulled me towards my mom's office, but my mom wasn't there. No one said, "Hey, kiddo," and no one told me everything was going to be OK.

We turned and ran down the Grand Staircase while the mansion transformed itself into a tomb.

"Cam, where's your mom?" Liz said, as if I knew but wasn't telling.

"Where are the teachers?" Bex said, spinning, looking in every direction. Tina and Eva came running down the hall. Mick, Kim, and Courtney came out of the Grand

Hall. Soon, almost the entire sophomore class was standing in the echoing foyer, but there were no teachers. No guards. The entire school must have been out, savouring their freedom in Roseville. We seemed to be entirely alone.

Then I saw a shadowy figure moving down the hall, stumbling, holding the wall to support himself.

"Mr Mosckowitz?" Liz yelled, then rushed forward with Bex.

Our teacher fell into their arms. Blood stained the side of his face, and his voice was faint as he lay on the floor and said, "He got it."

"Got what?" I asked through the roar of the sirens.

"The list – a disk with the alumni list." He sat up and gripped my shoulders. "He got it. And it's…out there."

And then Mr Mosckowitz passed out cold.

It's easy to look at the Gallagher mansion with its tall stone fences and ivy-covered facade and imagine the riches it must hold. Even people who know the truth about who we are and what we do probably think about the science labs where some of the world's greatest inventions have been born. Our library has been described as priceless. Still, our most precious resources aren't behind our walls at all – they're out in the world. Undercover. The real legacy of the Gallagher Girls lives not behind stone and glass but in flesh and blood. The other stuff – that's just for burn bags.

As we carried Mr Mosckowitz to a chair and checked his pulse, I couldn't shake the feeling that an entire sisterhood was riding on our shoulders.

The last rays of sunlight were disappearing from the mansion, so Tina pulled a lantern from the wall and struck a match. "Will somebody please tell me what's going on?" she demanded in frustration.

"The boys," I said. Even in the dark I could feel my friends looking at me, soaking in my every word. "Zach lied about seeing a tail in town – tails that were probably there to make sure we didn't come back too soon."

"And Mr Mosckowitz said *he* got the disk," Bex added.

"Which boy?" Mick asked. "How are we supposed to find him?"

That seemed like a very good question until I heard Liz beneath the roar of the sirens. "Well, it might be easier than you think."

She held out her hand, and for the first time I noticed that she wasn't wearing an ordinary watch. Instead, it was one of her custom designs. Tiny red dots on the screen shone like beacons in the dark. I thought back to our mission in the East Wing – the fingerprints, the DNA, and finally... Bex managed a triumphant grin. "We've got trackers."

Immediately we all turned and started outside, but stopped just as quickly. Steel covered every window and

237

every door. The very security measures that were supposed to keep intruders out were keeping us in.

"We can't get out," Tina said, dismayed.

Hope seemed to fade. The dot on Liz's monitor – the signal from the trackers we'd planted in the boys' shoes weeks ago – grew farther and farther away. I thought of my mom's advice, and I knew that, more than ever, I had to be myself.

So I looked at my friends. "Yeah," I said slowly, "we can."

I told myself that I'd been training my whole life for something like this – that we weren't as helpless as I felt, and for the first time that night my heart stopped racing; I took a deep, cleansing breath. Liz handed me her watch, and I peered down at the dots. Mick went in search of CoveOps essentials. Five minutes later we were pushing through cobwebs, smelling the dusty air of my favourite passageway.

Our flashlights cut through the black, and in the distance the sirens sounded like a stereo someone had left on.

I know those shadowy spaces – I can walk them in the dark. Blindfolded. In high heels. But this time something else lay at the end of the tunnel.

As the corridor branched and twisted, carrying us away from the mansion, I looked down at the monitor on my wrist and saw that most of the dots lay between the mansion and town – exactly where the boys were supposed to be. But one solitary dot moved away, so that's the signal – the boy – we followed.

When we exited the tunnel I saw the deserted highway that stretched out in two directions. The flashing dot went farther and faster as we stood there, unable to catch up.

"What now?" Liz asked.

"Anna, run around the perimeter until you reach the guardhouse – get help!" In a flash she was gone.

"Bex," I said, turning to my best friend; but just then my words failed me as I heard screeching tyres and saw headlights glowing. One of our vans drove fast in our direction then skidded to a stop. I breathed for the first time in what seemed like days, and relief washed over me. Help is here, I thought.

It was probably my mom.

Or Mr Solomon.

But then the doors flew open. And I heard Macey yell, "Get in!"

"You stole a Gallagher Academy van," I said, kind of amazed.

Macey shrugged. "Commandeered, Cam," she said. "When I couldn't get into the mansion, and heard the Code Black sirens, I *commandeered* a van. And yes," she said, as if reading my mind, "that's something that troublemaking debutantes learn how to do *before* they go to spy school."

Our headlights cut through the black. Mist fell from the sky – a warm, damp reminder that we'd come a long way since winter.

As we drove through the darkness, I didn't feel the rush of adrenalin that usually comes with covert operations. Instead of excitement, I felt a creeping horror that there had been a double agent in our midst. So I didn't let myself think about the boy I'd almost allowed to kiss me; I didn't dare wonder if I'd ever let myself feel that way again.

I turned up the sound on the monitor on my wrist, listened as a soft *beep, beep, beep* filled the van, faster than before, and I knew we were getting close.

"Turn here," I instructed, and the highway disappeared. We crept over gravel and potholes. "Hit the lights," I said. The van inched along in the dark.

The beeping was faster now, steady. "This is it," said Bex.

The clouds parted; a sliver of moonlight fell onto an industrial complex. Massive metal buildings stood clumped together. Weeds battled with gravel and broken bits of asphalt for control of the ground.

"What is this place?" Macey asked.

"It's an abandoned manufacturing company," Liz

explained. "But the school owns it now."

"It doesn't look like there's any security," Macey said.

And then every girl in the van said, "Look again."

Chain-link fence covered the perimeter. Probably a million dollars' worth of motion sensors lay imbedded in the ground. It was a fortress disguised as a ruin, and there wasn't a doubt in my mind that whoever we were following had come here for a reason.

"So we find whoever's in there and get the disk back?" Macey asked as if she isn't technically an Eighth Grader and two years away from Sublevel One.

"Yeah." I said.

"So I guess it's just like…" Bex started, but trailed off. "Just like last autumn?"

On an academic level she was right. It was like our autumn final. This was the same training ground, and we were still students, but as Mick started handing out comms units and Napotine patches, I couldn't help missing Mr Solomon and his cryptic pep talks, the clear-cut missions that outlined the difference between pass and fail.

I couldn't stop thinking that things weren't academic anymore.

Chapter 26

It's amazing how things come back to you – how instinct and training can take hold.

In an instant, Bex was disabling the van's tiny dome lamp so there would be no telltale spark when we opened the doors. Mick disabled the wires that charged the perimeter fence, and one by one we slipped beneath it, retreating into the distant corners of the complex, fading with the shadows and darkness and things that go bump in the night.

When you're approaching a subject in the dark, the thing you have to worry about most isn't being seen – it's being heard. And unfortunately, Liz was feeling chatty.

"Cam, I'm sure Zach's got a really good explanation. I just *know* he's not a bad guy." That was a nice sentiment – a hopeful thought – and I might have enjoyed it if Liz's foot hadn't been inches away from a nearly invisible trip wire that shimmered in the moonlight.

"Liz!" I hissed and leaped forward, pulling her to safety. "Why don't you wait here?"

"But…" she said, stumbling, sounding only slightly offended "Teamwork is key to covert operations."

"I know," I whispered as softly as possible. "But I need someone to stand here and watch this corner," I said, relieved to see a great hiding place behind an old barrel full of rain. "Can you do that?" I asked. "Can you stay right here and tell me if anyone comes this way?"

Even in the dark I could see the relief that flooded Liz's face. She was going to observe. It was maybe the most scientific assignment I could have given her, so she retreated into the shadows and I walked on alone, past puddles that lay under the eaves of the metal roofs, dodging stray cats and piles of forgotten lumber.

I walked through the maze of buildings, listening for anything louder than the sound of my own heartbeat. My head swam with questions: Where are they? Who are they? And above all, are we ready for this?

The Gallagher Academy's alumni list was probably inside one of those metal buildings – the identities of the world's top spies were spelled out in black-and-white. Lives were at risk; years of work could be undone. So even though I knew we were on our own, I still prayed that Anna would find help – that it wouldn't come too late.

The wind blew through the complex, howling between the buildings. I glanced down at the monitor on my wrist to make sure I was still moving in the direction of the solitary blinking dot. But this time the red dot was no longer alone.

I started to speak – to call out for my friends – but then I felt fingers clamp over my mouth. An arm was around my waist. And before I could take a step or throw a punch, I heard the hum of rappel-a-cord running through pulleys, and felt my feet leave the ground...

And the next thing I knew, I was flying.

"Cam," the voice near my ear whispered as we touched down on the roof of the building next to where I had been standing moments before. Wires ran between the surrounding rooftops. Harnesses and rappelling gear lay at my feet. And, on my wrist, Liz's old watch was blinking like crazy.

Without stopping to think, I stepped back into my attacker, tried to flip him over my head, but he countered his weight at that precise time, stopping my momentum. "It's me. It's Zach," he whispered, as if *that* were going to make me feel better.

A searchlight swept over the complex, beaming through the dark night, and automatically Zach and I dropped to the building's roof, laying ourselves flat as the light sliced above us.

"Give me one good reason why I shouldn't throw you off this building right now," I said, but the crazy thing wasn't that I meant it; the crazy thing was that I didn't *want* to mean it – that I wanted to believe in Zach; I wanted to like him and trust him and know that he knew the real me and liked me anyway.

I lay perfectly still, feeling the rough bite of the gritty tar paper on the palms of my hands.

"Give me one good reason why—" I started again, but Zach rolled towards me. His arm fell around my shoulders as his body pressed against mine.

"I'll give you two," he said, just as two armed guards walked around the corner in the exact same place I'd been standing moments before.

We lay in silence for twenty seconds, listening to the footsteps fade before I pushed myself away from him. "What's going on, Zach?" For the first time, I knew exactly what to say to him, and I wasn't afraid to say it.

"Who was that man in town?" I felt my fury rise. I twisted his arm behind his back and rolled him onto his stomach. "How did you find this place? Who is down there, and what are they going to do with the list?"

"Well, first of all, *ouch*," he hissed, but I didn't release the pressure. "Second, I came back to school after you ditched me in town with Jimmy—"

"Josh!" I snapped.

"I came back to the school after you ditched me –

245

thanks for that, by the way. Then it's all Code Black again and you and your whole class were gone. We figured you'd tracked us, so we tweaked the signal so we could follow your tracking mechanism. And here we are."

"Who's we?" I asked, gripping his arm tighter.

"Seriously, Gallagher Girl, that hurts like a – *ow!*" I twisted harder. "Grant, Jonas, some of the juniors. They're here, too. They're out there with your girls."

I looked over the side of the building and started to call a warning through the comms unit in my ear, but that one second of distraction was too much. Zach rolled. Then I was the one with my hands pinned.

"Cammie," he snapped, "look at me." I struggled and kicked, but he held tighter. "Gallagher Girl," he said gently, looking at me with the eyes of the boy who had almost kissed me – the guy who knew what it felt like to lose a parent. I'd spent a whole semester trying to find the *real* Zach, and that night, more than ever, I needed to know what was real and what was legend.

"You lied." My voice was soft, almost bruised. "I know you lied in town, Zach. I know you've seen that man who was on our tail."

"That's what this is about?" Zach exhaled a laugh. "You ditched me in town and organised a war party because I lied about knowing that guy?"

"No, I organised a war party because someone knocked Mr Mosckowitz out and stole the Gallagher

Academy alumni list!" I snapped. I could see terror register in Zach's eyes as he processed what was at stake. The pressure on my arms lessened. He wasn't holding me down anymore; he was just holding me.

And then something seemed to snap inside of Zach. He pulled my right hand in front of my face. "Here. Look at it." Until that moment I'd forgotten about the ring on my finger. "Or better yet, look at me. Watch my eyes, Cammie. I'm not lying." His pupils were even; his pulse was steady; and the truth ring stayed perfectly still as Zach explained, "I'd seen that guy with Dr Steve before and didn't want to blow his cover. I had no idea he was a threat. I thought he was on a training op or...I don't know...checking up on us or something. I didn't think it was a big deal." He shifted his weight and moved beside me. "I didn't think it was worth explaining in front of..." he trailed off, and I finished.

"Josh and DeeDee." I shook my head, trying to make sense of it all.

"We're not the bad guys, Gallagher Girl," he said gently.

More than anything I wanted to believe him. "Then who is?"

Zach let go of my wrists and pointed into the darkness. "Him."

One of the doors to the building across from us opened. I saw four armed guards walk out, and in the fleeting moment before the door closed, I heard a faint "Excellent," and saw the face of Dr Steve.

"Chameleon," Bex said in my ear. "Did you see that? Did you see who is in that big building? It's—"

"Dr Steve," I finished for her, and before I could say another word, I heard Eva cry, "Chameleon! The boys – they're here!"

"I know, Chica," I said, using Eva's code name. "Zach's with me."

"He is?" It was Liz. She sounded giddy.

"So that means Tina doesn't have to sit on Grant?" Eva asked.

"No. Tina needs to get off Grant." (Tina didn't sound at all happy about it.) "And bring him to the roof of the building on the northwest corner." I studied the boy beside me. "They've got some explaining to do."

For the next sixty seconds I heard my classmates making their way through the dark grounds, whispering to each other through the comms units as they cleared corners and ducked out of the sight of guards. The Gallagher Girls were coming, but for some reason, there, in the moonlight, with my sisterhood riding on everything I said and did, I found myself looking at Zach.

A few weeks ago, he warned me that I wouldn't want to sleep in his school, and now a semester's worth of cryptic messages and subtle hints had come down to this.

"What's going on, Cam?" Bex asked, as my classmates appeared beside me. She glanced at Zach. "Want me to throw him off the roof?"

"Only if he doesn't tell us what the Blackthorne Institute is and why one of their teachers is out to destroy the Gallagher Girls."

"What do you mean? You know what our school is," Grant said, as if the answer should be obvious. But it wasn't.

Their rooms were freaky clean; there was no trace of them in any record anywhere. They *weren't* like us – I'd known it all along. But Zach was the one to finally say, "You've got your cover. We've got ours."

"What's that supposed to—" I started, but Zach cut me off.

"You're Gallagher Girls," Zach snapped as the mist turned into rain. It streaked down his face, but he didn't blink; didn't back down. He just stepped closer and said, "We're the stepchild no one ever talks about."

I thought about the military precision of their rooms; the new uniforms; the way Zach had stood in the library and told me that he was neither all good nor all bad, and I knew there was more to the story.

"Then what—" I started, but the creak of rusty hinges cut me off; light sliced across the dark lot below as two armed guards left the building across from us and started to patrol the grounds. The question that had seemed so important moments before faded from my mind, and instead I said, "He can't get away. That list can't get away."

"It won't." Zach's words brought me back to another night when the Gallagher Girls stood in the same spot, on our way to rescue a hostage and a package.

This time the stakes were higher.

Zach walked to the edge of the roof and attached a rappelling harness to a cable that skirted down between the buildings, then reached for my hand. "We've got to go now, Cam." His gesture was like that of a gentleman asking a lady to dance. Madame Dabney would have been proud. "Do you trust me?" he asked, and I realised I had come full circle.

Months before I'd stood on that same roof with a different boy and leaped into the darkness towards my destiny.

But this time I wasn't jumping alone.

Chapter 27

Zach and I touched down on the stretch of grass that ran between the buildings, thankful for the rain, the clouds – for every trace of darkness Mother Nature could spare as I crouched low and ran through the space between the buildings.

"What are you *doing*?" Zach hissed, but I was already banging on the metal door that stood between me and Dr Steve. "Hey, can one of you guys come give me a hand with this?" I asked in the most manly voice I could muster.

Zach looked at me like I was crazy, but then the door opened and I pulled one of the guards out by his collar. Shocked and dazed, he didn't even realise what was happening as I knocked him out with one punch and slapped a Napotine patch on his forehead just to be on the safe side.

"Nice one," Zach said. "Did you learn that in P&E?"

"No. *Buffy the Vampire Slayer.*"

I studied the man who lay on the ground in front of us. The last time I'd seen him he'd been leaning against a 1957 Cadillac that stood parked along the Roseville town square. There was no telling how many operatives Dr Steve had helping him – I didn't want to think about the odds. I dragged the man to the tall weeds twenty feet away from the door and helped Zach go through his pockets.

"Comms," I said, pulling an earpiece and microphone off the sleeping man's body. Zach inserted the earpiece while I peered through the dusty windows.

Dr Steve was pacing the metal room. Crates lined the walls of the massive building, towering from the concrete floor to the tall ceiling.

"Guys," I whispered into my comms unit. "I've got a visual on the subject." At least four guards stood near Dr Steve. Every few steps he'd stop and pat his pocket as if making sure it hadn't been picked. "Maintain your position until we give you the all clear."

Zach leaned close to me. "They've got at least fifteen guys."

"What do you hear?" I asked. Zach held up a finger to shush me. A dark shadow crossed his face as he listened to what the enemy was saying. "What is it, Zach?" I demanded. "What's going—"

"Cammie, listen to me," Zach said. "I don't know

252

where he's going, or what Dr Steve's planning to do with that list, but…" Zach trailed off. His gaze left mine, and for a second it seemed to linger in midair, dwelling on some distant constellation. "I think I know how he's getting there."

He turned me to face west, where a small red light was blinking, growing closer.

"Guys," I whispered through my comms unit as the plane dipped lower on the horizon, "we've got a change of plans."

We were outnumbered and outsized. I heard the plane's landing gear groan as it started down, and saw the silhouettes of men exiting the building. This was not the time for a careful assault.

Bex jumped from the roof, flattening one guard, then swept a leg out and knocked a second one off his feet in one smooth motion. "They're here!" the man yelled out as he fell. But it was too late.

The buzz of rappel-a-cord through pulleys filled the air. For a moment it seemed to be raining Gallagher Girls. All around me fists flew, kicks landed. Zach touched the earpiece he'd stolen from the fallen guard and yelled to Bex and Grant, "Three guys are coming around the south side of the building – go!" And in a flash, they were off.

Liz had taken refuge in the cab of a forklift.

"Cammie, I need a weapon!" she called to me.

I'd knocked a guard to the ground and was struggling with a Napotine patch, but still managed to reply, "*You're sitting in one!*"

"Right," she said, and started looking for keys or a control switch – anything to make the big machine move. She must have given up, though, because the next time I saw her she was jumping from the cab, landing on the back of a guard who had been chasing Eva. The man spun around as if he couldn't quite imagine what had happened, and Liz squeezed tighter.

The plane touched down at the end of the runway. Through the rain, I saw the man in the blue jacket.

I moved towards him, feeling that things had got even more personal, but then the man Liz was gripping shook her free, and she went flying through the air, flattening the man in the blue jacket without throwing a single punch.

All around Dr Steve, the guards fell, one by one. To my right I saw a big burly guard go after Liz, but Zach lurched between them, taking a fist to the side of his face. He stumbled backwards, then caught my eye. He held his face with one hand and gestured to Dr Steve with the other.

"Go!" he screamed, and I ran.

The plane had reached the end of the runway; its propellers still spinning, a blur of water and light as the boys' teacher – our traitor – dashed through deep puddles and damp grass, bearing the straightest possible course towards the waiting aircraft – towards freedom.

I didn't think about my aching feet or growling stomach; I didn't hear the terrible thoughts that filled my head. I just put one foot in front of the other and ran until I stood just feet away from Dr Steve and the waiting plane. I could tell by the look on his face that nothing about that moment seemed "excellent" to him.

"I think you've got something that belongs to us," I said. My voice was steady and calm, maybe because of training, or nerve, or the sight of Bex inching along the ground, crawling through the tall weeds that rimmed the tarmac, until she was poised by the plane's back wheel. "You're not leaving with that disk," I said, feeling myself start to sway despite the adrenalin that coursed through my blood.

"Oh," Dr Steve said, as behind him the stairway to the plane began to descend. "I believe you're just a little…" He panted. "Too…" He drew another deep breath.

"Late." But this time Dr Steve didn't speak – he couldn't speak – because, take it from someone who has been the recipient of Rebecca Baxter's chokeholds, breathing is hard enough.

Dr Steve crumpled to the ground, and Bex went with him. The disk fell from his pocket, and I grabbed it. "You're not taking that anywhere." For the first time, I felt my energy fade. "You're not getting on that plane."

And then a voice behind me said, "That's right, Ms

Morgan, he's not." And I knew something was either very right. Or very wrong. But the one thing that was certain was that nothing was what it seemed.

I fully expected Mr Solomon to tell me to get out of the way because he was there with an elite special forces unit from Langley. I thought he'd handcuff Dr Steve or at least grab the disk and fly it away to safety. Instead he stepped lightly out of the plane and said, "Are you okay, Dr Sanders?"

"You," I said, barely recognising my own voice. "You did this?"

"Well," Joe Solomon said, "I had some help."

And then my mom came to join him.

I looked at the two of them, a thousand emotions brewing inside of me as my mom smiled at us and said, "Good job, everyone."

Even Dr Steve managed a smile. Well...as much of a smile as a guy in serious agony can muster.

"Rebecca?" Mom said. Bex loosened her grip. (She didn't totally let go, though.)

Mr Solomon looked at his watch. "Forty-two minutes," he said. "Not bad." He turned and called into the darkness. "What do you think, Harvey?"

Mr Mosckowitz stepped into the plane's open doorway – Mr Mosckowitz who had worn a fake moustache; Mr Mosckowitz who I had single-handedly tricked into untying me during my midterm final exam last autumn; Mr Mosckowitz, who was maybe the least seasoned field operative of the entire Gallagher Academy staff, smiled and bounced on the balls of his feet.

"Hi, girls," he said brightly. "How'd I do?"

Oh. My. Gosh.

The rain grew lighter around us. The pounding of my heart began to slow, and I felt my fears wash away and then get replaced by an emotion that I couldn't quite name.

"It…" I stumbled. "It was…a test?"

"Our job isn't to get you ready for tests, Ms Morgan," Mr Solomon corrected. "Our job is to get you ready for life."

I saw spotlights flash, felt the dim sky growing brighter and brighter, until the mist that hung in the air formed a massive rainbow over the abandoned buildings, the dark, empty lots. I watched the lights come on – in a lot of ways.

"So you wanted to see if we could do it for real?" Tina asked.

"No," my mom said. "We had to see if you could do it" – she looked at the boys and then at us – "together."

Our teachers turned and started through the rain towards the waiting vans while, behind us, the plane began to taxi down the runway, its lights fading in the distance.

I should have been happy. After all, the secrets of

my sisterhood were safe, and I'd just aced my CoveOps final.

Then Mr Solomon's voice called to us in the distance, "Oh…and welcome to Sublevel Two."

Chapter 28

There are tests for which even a Gallagher Girl can't study – no notes, no flash cards – just questions you have to answer every day; problems you must solve. I think it's probably true for any life – much less a spy's life – but that night as I lay in bed, listening to the play-by-play analysis in the common room down the hall, I couldn't shake the feeling that maybe the biggest test of the spring semester wasn't really over. I couldn't help but wonder if I'd really made the grade.

"Come on in, kiddo," Mom called as I reached the Hall of History the next morning – long before she could have seen me coming, because...well...my mom's kind of amazing like that.

Her office looked the same as always. Bright sunlight

streamed through the windows. The mahogany bookshelves gleamed. And my mom didn't look at all like a woman who had been up hours into the night. There were no bags under her eyes, no telltale traces of yesterday's makeup as she sat in the window seat, a file in her lap. "Are you angry?"

I don't know why the question stumped me, but it did. Though not nearly as much as the answer. "No."

I don't go to a normal school, and I've chosen not to have a normal life – normal tests aren't going to teach me the things I have to know, and the woman in front of me knew that better than anyone.

Mom scooted to the corner of the window seat, and I eased down beside her. "Was any of it real?" I resisted the temptation to ask what I really wanted to know: Were they real? Was Zach real?

I had begun that semester by sitting in the tower room, thinking about how spies don't tell lies – we live them – so it wasn't any wonder that I came to my mom's office that morning looking for some truth. I shouldn't have been surprised when the question I had carried with me the longest finally found a way to seep free.

"What happened to Dad?"

My mom's hand stopped running through my hair. The folder in her lap seemed to slip an inch or two, and I knew I'd broken one of the unwritten rules of the Gallagher Academy: I had asked to hear the story.

"You know what happened to Dad, sweetie."

But I *don't* know – and that's the problem. Give me a code and I can crack it; tell me a joke in Swahili and I'll know when to laugh. I know a million different facts in more than a dozen different languages… Just don't ask me when or where my father died.

I started to say all this, to ask the questions I need answered, but Mom straightened in the window seat. I felt her pull away. I found myself whispering Zach's words, "Someone knows."

Around us, the school was waking up. I heard laughter through the Hall of History. So I asked the other question that, so far, didn't have an answer. "Why this year?" I asked. "Why now?"

"I think you know the answer to that, sweetie."

And I guess I probably did because I said, "Josh."

"I don't know if you realise it, Cam, but what happened last semester…what happened between you and Josh…it scared a lot of people. It made us reexamine a lot of things."

"Do you mean security?" I asked. "Because I could really point out a blind spot or two they've missed."

"No, sweetie. Something bigger. We've spent millions training you girls with the best curriculum in the world. And yet you don't know much about half of the world's population." Which was true. "The trustees and I felt it was important that Gallagher Girls learn how to communicate with, and trust the men you'll have to work with some day."

Trust. We stake our lives on it, but it's a subject that not even the Gallagher Academy can teach. When do you let your guard down? Who do you let in? And I knew at that moment, as I sat beside my mom, bathing in the warm spring light, that those were the questions a good spy never stops asking.

Mom looked at me – and I could have sworn she was seeing straight through me. "If you hurry, you can catch him."

"Catch who?"

"Zach," Mom said. "The boys...the Blackthorne trustees want them to take final exams with their classmates." My mom must have sensed my confusion, because she said, "They're leaving."

"You're already packed," I said when I reached him, because, really, there wasn't anything else to say – or too much – I'm not sure.

He smiled. "We've all got baggage."

A crisp, clean breeze blew through the open doors. Breakfast was waiting. And classes. And finals. But the entire school seemed to be frozen in space and time. The boys carried suitcases and backpacks, while our world got ready to return to normal – whatever that's supposed to be.

I pointed to the bruise on his face. "That looks bad."

But Zach shook his head. "It isn't. He—"

"Hits like a girl?" I teased.

But Zach didn't smile; he didn't laugh. Something else hung in the air between us as he said, "Not the girls I know."

I thought about the boy I'd met in Washington – the kid who'd teased me all semester – and I tried to reconcile those images with the boy who stood before me.

Zach was still cocky; he was still tough. But on the other hand, he'd offered me chocolate once when I was hungry, and I couldn't help thinking that maybe that made him sort of knight-like after all. That maybe it wasn't his fault his armour was kind of tarnished.

A semester was gone, so I didn't let myself think about what might have happened if things had been different. After all, trust is a hard thing for any girl – especially a Gallagher Girl – and this is the life I've chosen. These are questions and doubts that will probably follow me for the rest of my life.

I turned slowly, started to walk away – towards my friends and my future and whatever was supposed to come next.

"Oh, and Cammie." At the sound of his voice I spun around, expecting to hear him crack a joke or call me Gallagher Girl. The *last* thing I expected was to feel his arms sliding around me, to sense the whole world turning

263

upside down as Zach dipped me in the middle of the foyer and pressed his lips to mine.

Then he smiled that smile I'd come to know. "I always finish what I start."

He stepped towards the open door and the warm spring sun that was just waiting to burst into summer, a new season. Another clean slate.

"So this is goodbye?" I asked.

"Come on, Gallagher Girl." Zach turned to me. He winked. "What would be the odds of that?"

He walked outside and got in the van, and as far as I could tell, he never looked back.

Because neither did I.

I didn't think about the rules we'd broken or the time we'd wasted. I didn't dwell on the questions that had seemed so important once and were now fading like a long-lost note in a heavy rain.

There are secrets in my world. They stack side by side like dominoes, and last September they'd started to fall – all because I'd said hello to a boy. Now I was saying goodbye to another one. But now, at least in Zach's case, I finally knew the truth. Well…most of the truth.

And it had set me free.

The whole summer lay ahead of us – time to rest, time to wait. And when the future comes – no matter what comes with it – I'll be smarter. I'll be stronger. I'll be ready.

**READ ON FOR A SNEAK
PEEK OF THE NEXT
GALLAGHER GIRLS BOOK,**

*Don't judge a girl
by her cover*

Chapter 1

"We're moving." The man beside me spoke into the microphone in his sleeve, and I knew the words weren't for me.

The August air was hot and thick with the smell of sea salt and bus exhaust. The roads were packed for miles, and everywhere I looked I saw shades of red, white and blue. Everywhere I turned, I felt the eyes of trained professionals staring, seeing, recording every word, analyzing every glance within a dozen miles.

Part of me wanted to break free of the big men in the dark suits who flanked me on either side; another part wanted to marvel at the bomb-sniffing dogs who were examining boxes twenty metres away. But most of all, I wanted to lie when another man, with a clipboard and an earpiece, asked for my name.

After all, I've spent a lot of time learning how to whip out false IDs and recite perfectly crafted cover stories in situations just like these, so it was harder than I thought to say, "Cammie. Cammie Morgan."

It was weirder than I would have guessed as I waited for him to scan the clipboard and say, "You can go right in."

As if I were simply a sixteen-year-old girl.

As if I couldn't possibly be a threat.

As if I didn't go to a school for spies.

Walking through the hotel lobby, I couldn't help but remember the first assignment my covert operations teacher ever gave me: *notice things.* Lights and cameras shone from every angle. A massive net full of red, white and blue balloons snaked through the cavernous space like a patriotic python. Up on the mezzanine level, the Texas delegation was singing about yellow roses, while a woman walked by wearing a big foam hat shaped like a Georgia peach.

I scanned the masses of old women and young girls. Husbands and wives. College kids and senior citizens. The last time I'd been in a crowd like this was in a different season and a different city, so maybe it was the hotel's frigid air-conditioning or just a memory of a chilly day in Washington D.C., but for some reason, I shivered and fought against a serious case of déjà vu as I looked around and said the name I hadn't spoken in weeks. "Zach."

Then I blinked and wondered if a part of me would always worry that he might be on my tail.

"This way," the man beside me said, but we didn't stop at the end of the line, which twisted and turned in front of the marble-covered registration desk. We didn't even slow down as we passed between two rows of elevators. Instead we turned down a narrow hall that seemed half a world away from the bright lights and tall ceiling of the lobby. Plush carpeting gave way to chipped linoleum tiles until finally we were standing before an elevator I'm pretty sure hotel guests were never intended to see.

READ

*Don't judge a girl
by her cover*

**TO FIND OUT WHAT
HAPPENS NEXT!**

Get to know your favourite author with our
Q&A with Ally Carter

How did you come up with Blackthorne?

I wanted Blackthorne to be the anti-Gallagher – some place with lots of secrets and shadows and a very unsavory past. To be a Gallagher Girl is kind of golden. Revered. But I wanted Zach to come from a place that is exactly the opposite. That is why the Gallagher Girls live in a mansion and Blackthorne is basically a prison.

I had a really hard time thinking up a name for the school. In fact, there is another name that even went out with the sales material for Cross My Heart way back when (a name I did not create and did not approve and, therefore, didn't stick around long).

Finally, one day I took a nap, because – seriously – I get my best ideas while napping. I'd always known I wanted it to start with a "B" (so that I could have the B-Boy alliteration like I have with Gallagher Girl). And as I was drifting off to sleep Blackthorne came to me.

The setting was inspired by my time at Cornell. Ithaca, New York is surrounded by lots of parks and areas with waterfalls. They were beautiful. And, of course, natural barriers and borders like that are in sharp contrast to the man-made borders they have at the Gallagher Academy. So, again, when in doubt, I just made everything at Blackthorne OPPOSITE of what you might have at Gallagher.

Do your characters ever do something that you didn't expect them to do?

Absolutely! All the time. There are a lot of things I know going into a book, but there are always even more surprises.

I didn't know Liz was renovating an old Dodge minivan. I never dreamed Bex and Zach were going to get super close when Cammie went away. I didn't even know Mr. Stein (in Heist Society) existed until Kat was knocking on his door.

Sometimes the writing just sort of takes over, and that is when you know the writing is going well.

Have you ever thought you met a spy?

I highly doubt it. But that probably just means I met a GOOD ONE!

What do you think about when you're alone in your car?

What do you think about when you're alone in your car?

I listen to the radio or audiobooks, and I think. Seriously, thinking is IMPORTANT. And I'm greatly concerned by how little time people spend just thinking anymore. Really. Truly. Put the cell phone down and THINK.
You will thank me for it.

Do you ever re-read your own books?

Not if I can help it. That sounds like my definition of torture

– reading something I can't fix if and when I find mistakes or things I just want to change. And, believe me, I would want to change things. All the things!

Who would make a better Gallagher Girl: Buffy the Vampire Slayer or Veronica Mars?

Probably Veronica. Buffy is tough and loyal and street-smart, but I think Veronica is probably a little more strategic, and that is probably more important in the life of a spy.

What's your favourite quote from one of your books?

I like the line from GG5 where Zach says, "Crazy. I went crazy."

I also like a line from Heist Society that goes something like "it is an occupational hazard that anyone who has spent their life learning how to lie will eventually become bad at telling the truth."

And lastly, if you could spend a whole day with one character from any of your books, who would you choose and why?

Ooh, good question! And a very hard one... I think I'd love to run around with Kat and Hale from Heist Society. As much as I love Cam and the Gallagher Girls, Kat and Hale just have a more (safely) exciting life. More chances to fly in a private jet with a hot boy...fewer opportunities to maybe be killed.

and

GOODY BAG GIVEAWAY

**10 randomly selected people who sign up
to our Ally Carter newsletter will win:**

★ A fabulous Miss Sporty make-up set worth £50!

★ Book 1 in the new-look Gallagher Girls series

★ An Ally Carter nail file

★ A new-look Gallagher Girls poster and bookmark

SIGN UP HERE, QUICK:
www.allycarterUK.com/comp

Deadline: March 31st 2015

Full terms and conditions can be found at the link above